JOIN ME IN DEATH

JOIN ME IN DEATH

SIDDHANT SHEKHAR

Vitasta

Published by
Renu Kaul Verma
Vitasta Publishing Pvt Ltd
4348/4C, Ansari Road, Daryaganj
New Delhi - 110 002
info@vitastapublishing.com

ISBN: 978-81-19670-74-1

First Edition 2024
MRP ₹ 399

Edited by Tanya Jain
Typeset & Cover Design by Rohit Gautam
Printed by Chaman Enterprises, New Delhi

Dedication

To my parents
for always nodding along
even when I didn't make sense

This world is a cruel place,
And we're here only to lose.
So, before life tears us apart, let
Death bless me, with you

-HIM

Prologue

This happened a year ago—12 April—I even remember the date. It's like it happened yesterday—it's so clear in my head.

It was around four in the morning, I think. The sky was black as ink, not a star in sight. No one would expect that, given I was just getting out of Shimla. The sky is clearer in the hills. You can see an entire range of galaxies, especially on no-moon nights like that one. But that night, nothing. It had been raining the entire weekend, my plans to go out and hit on Pahadi chicks was a wipe-out. The trip had been an utter waste of time. So, I was anyway pissed on my way back.

So, four in the morning. There were no vehicles on the road around me. I mean, who returns to Delhi on a Saturday night anyway, right? It was just me and my headlights for miles around, and in that condition, I had to pee.

Now, I know, it was an incredibly stupid idea. Dark road, no one around for miles, I was alone in my car, everything around seemed to be screaming at me to hold it till I get to the next settlement. But when you gotta go you gotta go. So, I found a straight stretch and stopped my car on the side of the road.

I got out and it was pitch black all around me. You couldn't see shit. I left the headlights on but that was barely of any help. I went a few feet off the road, towards the edge and faced some bushes. Thankfully, it was not a steep drop behind them, but would have still been a climb for anyone.

I finished my business and suddenly, I felt like someone was watching me. You know that feeling right? The hair on the back of your neck stand up. Your heartbeat quickens for no reason. It was the middle of the night. It could be a wild animal for all I knew. So, I hurried to finish and zip everything back up and began to pace quickly towards the car.

I would have hardly taken couple of steps maybe, when I heard a rustling from the bushes. I spun around, purely on instinct, pull out my phone and switched on the flashlight. Nothing. It was all quiet. I turned towards my car again and this time there was a clear rustling from behind me, as if something was stalking me. I picked up a stone and walked backwards slowly towards my car, as silently as I could. The rustling stopped and all of a sudden, a hand shot out.

I swear to you, that was the most afraid I had ever been in my life. Like think of the most scared you have been—swerving motorcycle, your parents finding you having sex in their bedroom, whatever it is, it was nothing compared to what I felt in that moment. I could feel my stomach drop, like physically drop a few inches.

I turned and ran for my life. You know the cliché they

show in the horror movies? Like people trip over nothing when running away from a serial killer? Absolutely true. When you are that scared your signals, all get scrambled, and you start tripping on your own feet. I tripped on something on the ground and my phone flew like ten feet from me, with the torch's side downwards. So now, the only light on the entire road was from the headlights, facing away from where I was.

I crawled like a mad man and got into the car. Thankfully, I had left the doors unlocked so I yanked them open, fell in and locked myself inside. I fished out the keys from my pocket to start the car, but my hands were trembling so badly I couldn't get it into ignition. I heard a loud thud from the back of the car, as if someone was pounding the trunk hard. The car began to move up and down from the force of it. I looked in the rear view and saw a woman there. She was dressed in white, her face was streaked in blood, her hair were all over the place and she was beating on the trunk. I swear to you, I nearly shit myself just at the sight.

Just then, the key slipped into ignition. I twisted the keys, but the car refused to start. The engine coughed and spluttered. I saw the figure moving forward, to the passenger side's gate, yanking at the door handles. I turned the key again and this time, the engine roared back to life.

I pressed the pedal so hard that the wheels spun in the dirt like they do in the cartoons. The car lurched forward and I swerved onto the road. I kid you not, I heard a scream from behind me. I glanced at the rear-view mirror and I saw the figure in white become smaller and smaller yet running after me. I gunned forward and I am serious, I drove at a speed of about hundred on those mountainous, hair-pin roads for atleast the next hour until I found a dhaba and a petrol pump.

Chapter 1

'And that is the true story of how I saw a ghost,' Aryan Sinha completed his story conspiratorially, beaming at the reaction he had received.

'You are lying,' Priyanka spoke in dismissal. However, the quiver in her voice was not lost on Aryan.

'I swear, I am not. It was not even that far from here. Some hundred kilometres maybe. I will show you the spot on our return trip on the bus. Why do you think I took the bus this time? I am not getting into a car alone on these roads ever again.' Aryan insisted, with the hint of a mischievous smile on his lips.

'Nope, you are still lying,' Priyanka made a face and stuck out her tongue.

Aryan shrugged, smiling, fully aware that he had just won the campfire horror story tradition. He hugged himself, pulling his shawl tighter around him. Even though it was May, it was nippy out there, some four thousand feet above sea level. He could see the shapes of the lower Himalayan peaks faintly out in the distance despite the darkness. They were some twenty of them, on a trek to Hampta pass.

Aryan stood up and walked off slowly, letting the shawl fall from him. He was tall—taller than average—at six feet. The jacket and warm clothes hid that, but he was in reasonably decent shape, having been blessed with a metabolism that didn't turn air to fat. He was also an athlete in college, sprinting and running the occasional two mile and he carried that with him, even out of college. His three-times-a-week five-km runs had made sure that despite working a desk job, he did not develop the soft belly that most corporate rats usually did.

The most striking thing about him was his face though—clear, smooth skin, with a chiselled jawline. His eyes were the perfect distance apart, set with a micrometre scale. He got a single dimple on his left cheek when he smiled and would have been considered conventionally attractive without much effort even on his worst day.

'Aryan?'

Aryan paused and turned to see Priyanka walking up meekly to him. She was cute, he decided.

'Yes?'

'That story. The one that you just told us. Was it true?' Priyanka spoke slowly, finally able to shed the brave face she had to put up in front of the group.

Aryan fought back a smile, unsure of whether it would be appropriate to laugh right now.

'What do you think?'

'It doesn't matter what I think. You tell me. Did it really happen?'

'You want to know what really happened?'

Priyanka nodded weakly.

'Take a walk with me. I will tell you what happened.' Aryan spoke with an encouraging smile on his face, holding out a hand to Priyanka, gesturing towards the stream.

ARYAN yawned loudly as soon as the city came into view. He had done exactly what he did not want to do—did not get enough sleep the night before, walked down the hills like a zombie, crashed into people and trees, and then passed out the second he got on the bus, forgetting all his plans to click pictures of the valley.

He turned in his seat and caught Priyanka staring at him. As soon as their eyes met, she looked away, pretending to look out of the window, reddening ever so slightly. Aryan grinned to himself, pulling out his headphones and journal.

He had always been a gifted artist, even getting a job as an animator in an advertising firm without much formal training. Sure, digital art was quicker and easier to share and modify and all that, but there was just something magical about graphite on paper. He felt like it connected him to the long line of artists that had come before him—Vinci, Raja, Husain.

The bus jerked to a halt at the market in Manali. Aryan cursed as the jerk made him stretch his last stroke over the entire sheet, making it look like a hastily struck through reject. He tried to salvage it, seeing if he could incorporate the line into the drawing somehow, but gave it up as a bad job.

He got down from the bus, stretched, still mumbling

angrily to himself. He turned to see Akshay, his colleague and partner on this hike, scratching his head sleepily and waddling towards him.

'Why did we think it was a good idea to take the bus and not our car?' Akshay said, massaging his neck.

'Dude! Come on! I told you the story. There are ghosts around here.'

'Oh, fuck off! As if I haven't seen you use that story a thousand times to get laid.'

'Well, oops?' Aryan laughed out loud. He turned to see Priyanka looking at him from a distance and quickly turned his gaze.

'Come on. I need some coffee. What time is the bus back?' Akshay asked, starting to walk towards the market.

'Eight. We have the day to kill. Let's do something.' Aryan spoke excitedly.

'Yes! Let's find a place with a real bed and die on it till it is time to get back on the bus.'

'Urgh! What is wrong with you? Once we get back to Delhi it will be the same old routine all over again. The same old cubicle, the same old clients, and the same old deadlines. Let's do something fun today.' Aryan tugged on Akshay's jacket.

'Here is the thing. I might die of boredom once I return to being a corporate slave, but I will definitely die today if I don't get some real sleep.'

'Go die! I will meet you at the bus station. Here, take my bag with you. I am gonna explore the city,' Aryan slung his bag off his shoulder and handed it to Akshay.

'Cool. Don't be late.' Akshay yelled behind the diminishing figure of Aryan.

ARYAN stopped at a small cafe in Mall Road, the main street of Manali. It was the home of the district administration buildings but was dominated by shops and cafes that speckled both sides of the road. He had a light breakfast of eggs, toast, bacon and coffee and set out to explore the city.

Manali, like most other hill stations, was dependent on tourism for its economy. A small town by Indian standards, of just over fifteen thousand people, it was a major producer of Apples and Trouts, the latter introduced to the region by the Britishers. Aryan regretted forgetting his camera with his luggage that he had given to Akshay but clicked some pictures nevertheless on his phone. He planned on using these as models for sketches on his way back.

After roaming around for a few hours, Aryan reached the edge of the city and sat down in front of a small shack. It was away from the din of the city square, and Aryan liked the solitude. He had just spent the last three nights sharing a tent with Akshay on the trek and was really looking forward to going back to his own room, where he could finally have some alone time.

He straddled the bench he was sitting on and raised the earthen cup of chai, a *kulhad*, to his lips. The hot, slightly spicy tea traced its way down his chest, immediately warming him up.

There were mountains on all sides. The shack was on one side of a gravelly, uneven road that led away from the city. Beyond the flimsy metal railing installed to prevent accidents, the ground quickly dropped about thirty feet. At the bottom of this small valley, a clear, glass-like stream of water snaked languidly. Aryan's eyes traced the stream back up the small waterfall it was coming from and he could clearly hear the gurgle of the stream at the drop off point despite the distance. There was enough time to go sit with his feet in the stream for a while before he headed back to the city to take his bus. Paying the shopkeeper with a fifty rupee note, Aryan half-walked, half-stumbled down, his feet unsure on the rocky terrain of the slope to the stream.

Sliding and slipping, Aryan reached the bottom of the slope, where the ground flattened out. It was covered in pebbles, perfect for skimming if only he knew how to. He took off his shoes and walked slowly to the stream barefooted, careful to not step on pieces of trash the tourists had so graciously left for him. He entered the water slowly, wincing. It was cold.

He had taken only a few steps when he heard a voice behind him at a distance. He turned to see a girl, climbing back up the slope, the way he had come. She looked young, maybe his age, or a few years older at most, dressed in a light blue parka and thick hiking boots covering her feet. She had long hair, Aryan could tell from the distance, and for a second he stood there, suddenly longing for some company.

The crack rang out as sudden as a whip. The girl had

stepped on a loose stone and slipped, pretty badly by the looks of it. Aryan ran towards her, unsure if he would make it there in time. If the girl took a tumble, it was a nasty fifteen foot fall. It wouldn't kill anyone but it sure wouldn't tickle either. He dropped his shoes to the ground as soon as he stepped out of the water and slid his feet in. It wasn't comfortable but it would do. He needed the grip to climb up. Within a few seconds, he was right underneath her, as she hung onto a shrub to balance herself and was trying to get back to her feet.

'Hey! Are you okay?' Aryan yelled out.

The girl turned to look at him and slipped a few inches further, letting out a startled yell.

'Just hold on. I'm coming,' Aryan put on his shoes and laced them up tightly. He looked around for a stick but couldn't find any so started climbing with just his hands and feet.

'Here, give me your hand.' Aryan said, once he had reached the girl.

The girl looked at his feet, her eyes still wide in fear.

'Don't worry. I have a good spot. I won't fall. Give me your hand.'

She let go of the bush with one gloved hand and extended it to Aryan. He slowly grabbed it, and planting his feet squarely, pulled in one smooth motion. The girl found her feet and stepped up. The loose gravel under her feet rolled down innocently as she steadied herself with Aryan's support and stood up.

'Are you ok? Haven't twisted your foot, have you?' Aryan said, with concern in his voice.

'No, I don't think so. I just slipped. Thanks.'

'Don't worry about it. You are going back up?'

'Yeah.'

'Cool, let's go back up together then. The rains have made the trail slippery.'

They climbed back up slowly, holding hands to steady each other. It was a slow climb, and it took them nearly ten minutes to reach the tea shack. They heaved their way back to the top, Aryan leading the way, but more so in his head than in reality. The girl was much lighter on her feet than him.

They sat at the tea shack, on opposite benches. Aryan did not want to stare, so he busied himself with looking around, pretending to be really interested in the stream he was just sitting by.

'Thanks,' the girl's voice rang out after a few strained, awkward seconds of silence.

Aryan turned to look at her, noticing for the first time how pretty she was. She had a round face, with big, black eyes and shoulder length hair that curled at the end. She was dressed simply in a parka, leggings and hiking boots and wore (what looked like to him) no makeup. She did not seem to have any luggage with her, not even a small purse that all women he knew carried at all times.

'Don't worry about it. Good thing I ran into you. Climbing back up on my own would have been tricky.'

'Yeah. I suppose. Hi, I'm Rashmi, Rashmi Agarwal.'

'Aryan. Aryan Sinha.'

They shook hands and got up to leave.

'Are you from here?' Aryan asked, sensing she was about to leave.

'Uh, no. I am from Delhi. I came on a camping trip with my friends.'

'Oh! No kidding! So did I.'

'Oh! That's nice,' the girl offered politely, with the restraint that all women must practice while talking to a stranger for the first time.

'Yeah. So, are you heading back into the city?' Aryan asked.

Rashmi turned around. It wasn't dark yet but given how winding hilly roads were, it would be by the time she reached the city.

'Yeah, I guess so. I want to get back before it gets dark.'

'Yeah, makes sense. How did you get here?'

'I walked.'

'Hmm. Want to walk back? I'm going that way too.'

'Erm. Yeah, no. Maybe.'

'Well, those are the options.' Aryan laughed out, his heart thumping in his chest.

Rashmi laughed politely. She tucked her hair behind her ear with a finger and bit her lip, unsure of what she should do.

'Alright, sure. Let's walk back,' she replied after a few seconds.

'Great. After you. And I mean that literally. Because I have no idea where I am.'

'Off to a great start, aren't we?'

For the first time, both of them, laughed together.

Chapter 2

'So, you're an animator, huh?' Rashmi smirked.

'Yup. Started going to a college for it, but got bored and quit midway. Then, I began with doing small little projects of my own, and a few months later, the guys at Olint offered me a job. I have been with them since.' Aryan replied.

'Wow! It sounds amazing,' Rashmi offered with a polite smile.

'Well, it's not too bad.'

They strolled up the road leading to the city centre. It was one of the peculiarities of the hill towns. Only two directions existed, up and down. No one dealt in those feeble compasses, or flimsy maps. Everywhere you had to go was either up or down. They stopped to ask a few times, and all the good Samaritans had directed them in the laconic, vague for tourists, vocabulary of up and down.

It was starting to get dark, and they were still about a good half hour's walk from the centre of the city, where Aryan would catch his bus back to Delhi. The air had gotten cold and both of them had zipped up their jackets. Aryan wasn't too happy about it.

'So, what about you?'

'Oh, nothing that exciting. School, engineering college, got a job in my final year, been working a standard nine to five job since. Very boring compared to you.'

'Well, it sounds fancier than it is. Half my time is spent deciphering whatever my client meant by "It's not jazzy enough!". It's like they avoid usable instructions like the plague.'

'I know what you mean,' Rashmi smiled, 'But you can't blame them, either. No one in the country gets an education in art. Well, no one who didn't already want one. Most of the good places are out in the West, because I often talk to people from there, they have courses in their schools about art history and appreciation. That vocabulary doesn't exist here because no one is taught that. So, you end up with people who only vaguely know their own artistic sensibilities and can't explain why they like or dislike anything. Am I making sense?'

'Of course. Better than I could have put it myself,' Aryan smiled. Rashmi smiled back at him and increased her pace.

'Hurry up, I want to reach the city before it's dark out.'

'Yeah, I don't trust the hills in the dark myself. Crazy stuff,' Aryan started, setting himself up for his story.

'I know,' Rashmi replied, shooting him down.

They reached the centre of the city just as the street lamps were heating up. They bathed the city square in a warm, orange glow. Tourists and hawkers were milling about on the streets. Couples were looking for good spots to click pictures, hawkers were trying to sell roses to them, that the men would be pressured into buying, even though the women didn't want them either. Aryan looked around for the bus and saw a row of them parked on a road some distance away from the city square.

'What time are you leaving?' He turned to Rashmi.

'Four in the morning. We have a car. We already let go of our rooms. Our plan was to roam around the city at night. Go hang out at a twenty-four seven cafe or something like that and then leave early in the morning.'

'Where are your friends?'

'I don't know. Must be around here somewhere. I am supposed to meet them around ten there, in front of that cafe with all the flags.'

'Ok,' Aryan nodded slowly, 'So I have a couple of hours to kill. Do you want to grab a drink?'

'No.'

'Oh,' Aryan's face fell.

'Some coffee would be nice though,' Rashmi replied, looking mischievously in the distance, trying to suppress a smile.

Aryan's face broke into a wide grin. He had not struck out! Not yet. His boyish charms still had their magic!

'Of course. Do you know a place? I need to eat too.'

'Sure. I think I know a spot. I found it last year with my friend Roy. He is a bartender in Hauz Khas Village and is super into these quirky places. Do you like Tibetan food?'

'It's like you are reading my mind.' Aryan spoke, staring right at Rashmi.

A few minutes later, they were settled comfortably in a small, home style cafe overlooking the city square. A small house had been converted into an eatery, with tables and chairs laid out in a neat square grid on the verandah. The place was lit up dimly, mostly with yellow, fairy lights and little incandescent bulbs hanging from the ceiling precariously. The railing was covered in lights and a wall on the other end was plastered with yellow and pink post-it notes and a few polaroids. The speaker overhead was playing an old Hindi song, *Naina Barse Rimjhim Rimjhim*. Aryan pulled out his smartphone and began shooting a video of the cafe. Just as he was turning the camera towards Rashmi, her voice rang out.

'Oh God! Put that phone away, will you?'

'What? What's wrong with it?'

'Don't tell me you are one of those people who must document everything happening to them to feel that it is real. You are here, this is happening, isn't that enough?'

Grinning, Aryan put away his phone and joined Rashmi at the table. He saw, she had pulled out a pen, and was doodling on the napkin.

'Hey! You are pretty good!' Aryan remarked.

'What? This? This is nothing. It's just something I do when I have some time free.' Rashmi said, crumpling the napkin in her palm and dropping it on the floor.

Aryan dived to pick it up, dodging Rashmi's attempts to flick it away. He smoothed it out on the table and looked at it. It was an intricate pattern or lines and curves, reaching all the way to the end of the napkin.

'This is great!'

'No, it's not,' Rashmi replied, slightly embarrassed.

'Come on! What are you talking about? This is amazing.'

'Well, I'm not a professional like you?'

'So?'

Rashmi fell silent. She did not have an answer. She stared at the napkin, avoiding Aryan's gaze.

'You know it's something that has happened in recent years,' Aryan spoke after a few moments of silence.

'What?'

'This need to monetize all your art. And discard whatever you cannot.'

'What do you mean?'

'Think about it. You enjoy doing this, making these, for the lack of a better word—doodles. You could have been doing anything right now. But instead, you chose to do this. And now you are pretending it is worthless only because I do art for a living, and you don't. But that doesn't mean what you were doing is less than what I do in any way.'

'I'm listening,' Rashmi said, her head tilted to the side.

'There was no market for cave paintings. There were no museums holding exhibitions of paintings of people killing bisons. But our ancestors did it anyway. Why? Because it made them happy. But now, anything you do, if you can't make money from it, is rejected as worthless. Why can't someone who enjoys doing something just do it for the sake of it anymore? We have somehow managed to commoditise art. Where everyone should have been an artist, there are professionals now, and you are supposed to consume their art, which is supposedly superior to what you do. Why? Why can't both of us be artists? Doing something that we enjoy.'

'Point well made. I agree. Give me that,' Rashmi reached for the napkin, with a broad smile on her face.

'Why?' Aryan snatched the napkin out her reach on instinct.

'Well, because I have to finish it. It's not done yet,' she replied with a grin.

Smiling, Aryan returned the napkin. Just as she was taking it, their fingers touched and a bolt ran down Aryan's spine. Her fingers were cold as ice.

Rashmi returned to her doodle, and Aryan looked around.

'Hey! I have an idea.' Aryan said.

'What?'

'Let us both make portraits of each other. Whoever does a better job, gets an extra slice of apple pie.'

'You are on!'

Aryan pulled up a napkin and a pen he always carried with himself and got to work. They both sat silently drawing, the music crooning softly over them. The wind from the valley was cold, Aryan could feel them cutting through his fingers. He held the cup of coffee in his other hand and was grateful for the warmth. He stole glances at Rashmi every now and then to see her diligently at work on her napkin, her tongue sticking out from a corner of her mouth like a little child concentrating on her alphabets. The yellow light caught her from one side and blinking lights from the valley made her look even more beautiful. The whole thing looked like a scene from a movie that Aryan was delighted to be a part of.

'Done!' Aryan declared about ten minutes later.

'What? Already? How? Is it one of those things where you just made a stick figure of me?'

'What? No! Here, take a look,' Aryan slid the napkin across the table.

Rashmi looked at the napkin, speechless. Aryan was rather proud of it too. It was amazing. It caught every curve of her face. The delicate turn of her chin, her eyelashes that were a bit too short, the way her nose ended abruptly, like a cliff falling into the sea.

'Well, fine! Enjoy your pie!' Rashmi replied, with a mock pout.

Aryan laughed out loud. He found her tantrum endearing.

'Keep it. It will remind you of me.'

'Well, I'll be damned if I need this to remember you.' Aryan spoke with a wink and saw Rashmi turn just a shade pinker.

They ate in silence, partly because the food was too hot and partly because now there was a tension that Aryan could feel wasn't there earlier. He even caught Rashmi stealing glances at him when she thought he wasn't looking. Feeling slightly pleased with himself, he looked intently into his *thukpa*, letting the tension build.

'What time is it?' Aryan said, pulling out his phone, now the table in front of them looked like a battlefield, the final resting place of many valiant roosters and lambs.

'Twenty to eight.'

'Well, damn.'

'What time do you have to leave?' Rashmi asked, looking at the clock on the wall.

Aryan should have left ten minutes ago. But he did not want to. All of it, the meeting, the coffee, the conversation, it all felt ethereal to him. He felt drawn to her for reasons he could not figure out. She was not the prettiest girl he had seen, nor was she coming onto him. But there was something that held him by the hand and did not let him leave. Something beyond the physical, maybe even the emotional.

'I am not going.'

'What?' Rashmi shot back.

'Yeah. I am not going. I am staying here with you.'

'Are you mad? Go! You will miss your bus.'

'It's fine. I'll go tomorrow evening. I have the day off anyway.'

'Don't be an idiot. GO!' Rashmi said forcefully, her face severe now.

'Ok. I am an adult. I know what I am doing. Get off my back.'

'I have to go at ten too.'

'Fine. I am not stopping you.'

'God what's wrong with you? You are making me feel bad.'

'If I left right now, I would feel worse.'

Rashmi fell silent, unsure of how to respond.

'You remember what you said earlier? About something being real and happening right now? It is happening right now. And I don't want it to end so quickly. I am not asking you for anything. I just want to spend some more time with you, that's all.'

'Are you sure?' Rashmi finally spoke, after a few seconds.

'I have never been more sure of anything in my life. I already texted my friend too. He will keep my stuff, I'll pick it up from his place.'

'Ok,' Rashmi replied, her face breaking into a wide smile now, that no one could misunderstand.

'I'll text my friends too. What should I say? Is this fine?'

Aryan squinted at the screen. It was a text to someone named Sneha and it said "Hey! I will see you guys later. Don't wait for me."

Aryan's face broke into a grin too as they both sat across the small square table, suddenly aware that something was happening here.

'So, now that we are here. Another coffee?' Aryan said.

Rashmi smiled and nodded.

Aryan looked around the city square to see the whole city pack up and go home, like it had a life of its own and just like any of us, needed its sleep. It was a little over nine when they left the cafe and went out for ice cream in the city square. Most of the shops had closed, but the ice cream sellers persisted, catering to the market of night time cravings the world over. They walked in circles around the square, casually strolling from one end of the paved street to the other, talking the entire while as if the rest of their lives depended on it.

'You know, it is not like I have not done crazy things

before,' Rashmi said, her eyes locked with Aryan, 'In fact, more than I can count. But now I feel like I am over all of that, you know? Like I have somehow evolved beyond making those choices and looking back at them, I am not sure why I made them in the first place.'

'I know what you mean. When most of my friends were out partying and going crazy, I was cooped up in my room working ten hours a day building my portfolio and delivering projects to clients as a freelancer. Sure, it helped me and I am grateful for all of that, but what I missed out on for that early start, I will never get a chance to experience again. I will never be nineteen in Delhi again, I will never be twenty going for a date in Hudson Lane ever again. I just feel like somehow, I missed out on my youth. I sort of just turned into an adult directly from being an adolescent...'

As Aryan heard the words he was speaking, he was surprised at how much of himself he was baring to this girl he had met only a few hours ago. These were thoughts, fears, insecurities that no one knew about, possibly not even himself because he had never managed to articulate them. But here he was, in the middle of the night, in a sleepy little hill station, talking like it was going out of fashion with a stranger. Who somehow, miraculously, understood. He did not fear judgement, or that he would be considered less of a man for not having it all together. He instead wanted to share things with Rashmi and wanted to hear what she thought about them. Tell her that he felt this too and somehow he was not crazy for feeling this way.

The words flowed out of their tongues like a river breaking through a dam. There was no restraint, nothing that was off the table. They talked about their childhood, things they remembered from back then, things that shaped them into who they were today. They talked about their family, who despite all the love drove them crazy with their concern and how it would be nice to have them take themselves a little less seriously at times. They acted silly, talking in funny accents, about people they had met on their journeys, the eccentric professor, the weird classmate, the awkward yet fiercely loyal friend.

The more he found out about Rashmi, the more he was startled at how different her perspective towards the world was. She was more trustworthy, more optimistic, and believed in the goodness of people. Aryan had lost that a few months into his freelance career. He found himself wanting to protect Rashmi more and more as she said things that he knew were not true. It was not how the world worked and he found out the hard way. But there was an innocence in her perspective too. There was wonder, and joy, and curiosity that Aryan envied her for. He wanted to look at the world the way she did, as he had too, once upon a time.

Around 1 am in the night, when they were tired of walking, they asked around and found a midnight cafe which served food. Though they had been talking for hours, neither of them felt like they had run out of things to say. If anything, they were going down deeper and further into the reaches of their own minds.

They had a simple meal of noodles, followed by brownies and sat back in the cafe, too tired to walk now. Their eyes were red, and Aryan could hear the drowsiness in his own voice as well. He knew that if he stopped talking, he would most definitely fall asleep.

'How are you guys going back?' Aryan broached the subject as four ticked closer. He did so reluctantly, afraid that mentioning the morning after would make this night end and he was not ready for that.

'We have a designated driver and a car. Don't worry. I'm not driving,' Rashmi replied, suppressing a yawn, setting Aryan off too.

'I want to take a picture.'

'No!' For the first time, there was firmness, maybe even anger in Rashmi's voice.

'What happened? Did I say something wrong?'

'I don't want to take a picture please. Put your phone away.'

'Come on! What's wrong with it? I won't make you look bad. I promise.'

'Please Aryan. Don't insist. I don't want to. Understand.' Rashmi said softly now, almost pleading with him.

'Well then how I am supposed to tell people what I was doing the entire night.'

'You need a picture to remember this night? Well, that's disappointing.'

'You know it's not true,' Aryan laughed, 'I won't take a picture, fine. But I still don't see what the big deal is.'

'I have my reasons. Please.'

'Ok.'

A silence fell between. Tense. It felt like Aryan had been shaken rudely awake from a dream that he was having and no matter how tightly he closed his eyes, he could not go back to it.

'It's almost time. I should leave now.' Rashmi said, getting up gingerly.

'I'll drop you.' Aryan started to rise too, pulling out his wallet to pay the bill.

'Don't bother. You are tired. Go get some sleep. You need it badly; I can see that.'

'It's no big deal, I can drop you.' Aryan said, trying to suppress an ill-timed yawn.

'Relax. It's right around the corner. Do you have the portrait you made of me?'

'Yeah. Why?'

'Give it here.'

Aryan pulled it out of his pocket, puzzled. Rashmi picked up a pen from the table and scribbled her number on it.

'Give me a call once you reach Delhi. We will meet.'

'Like a date?'

'Sure,' Rashmi laughed, 'like a date. Alright. I will take your leave now. You take care. And call me once you reach Delhi.'

'Take my number too then.'

'I will just lose it. Don't worry, I trust you.' Rashmi smiled.

Rashmi leaned in for a hug. Aryan could smell her hair. They did not smell of anything fruity, or citrusy, like a shampoo. They smelt like what in his head Aryan had always imagined hair would smell like. He breathed in deeply, unwilling to let go.

'Thank you for tonight. No matter what happens, we will always have this.' Rashmi gently whispered in his ears.

Aryan let go and watched Rashmi pick up her jacket and put it on. He wanted to say something, maybe just a goodbye, but words got stuck inside him. He just kept watching her walk away, through the door, down the stairs, across the street. The slamming of the door brought him back to his senses and he chased after Rashmi, to kiss her goodbye. He sprinted down the stairs, nearly tripping over the last step, and broke through the door.

An empty street mocked him. Rashmi had vanished into the morning mist.

Chapter 3

A few weeks passed and Aryan fell into a daily routine. He would wake up, call the number, hear the lady coldly telling him that the number he was trying to reach was switched off, punt his phone across the room, get ready, go to work, return, have his dinner, call the number, hear the same thing all over again and go to sleep dejected. He hated teetering on the edge of hope and despair. He knew maybe no one would ever pick up the call but he could not get himself to stop calling.

The people around him noticed it too. The outgoing Aryan, one who never said no to a party, stopped accepting invitations to go out, or even to hang around watching a match over beers. He let his calls go unanswered often, especially between five and seven in the evening, when he knew the call would inevitably be an invitation to go out and do something. He even uninstalled all the dating apps on his phone, much to the dismay of the fair ladies of the great city of New Delhi.

New Delhi—what a city to be alive in! It did not have

the pretence and the frantic pace of Mumbai and the distance and needless sophistication of Bengaluru. It was a city, which since the beginning of time invited all with open arms. It took in refugees and invaders, the poor and hungry and the rich and powerful—all the same. If you came to plunder its wealth, or to escape the poverty of a failed state, the city did not care. It made you its own, nursing you with history and a life that was not the one you imagined but one you could not complain about. It did not hate you if you came from someplace else, if the colour of your skin was unusual. It gave you a roof over your head and a street to call your own and watch it change as the years passed by. It took all the mean things that were said about it, smiled at them, and lived on the way it wanted to. It gave you permission to be obnoxious. There were few things that fazed it. Empires rose and fell, regimes and ideologies came and passed away, but the city lived on.

'For crying out loud, will you stop moping around? People are starting to think that someone died,' Akshay said in irritation one evening, he found Aryan sitting around the office, staring at the black screen of his phone.

'What?' Akshay's head jerked up, as if broken out of a trance.

'Ok, that's it. You are coming with me tonight.'

'No man. You carry on. I am not in the mood.'

'Oh, I am sorry. You thought that was a request? You are coming with me, end of story. Get off your ass.'

'Dude, please. Come…'

'Are you kidding me? Will you look at yourself for a second? You met a girl one time, and she ditched you. Big deal! Get over it! I am not watching you mope around for the rest of your fucking life.'

Aryan looked at his face in the dark glass in front of his cubicle overlooking the city. It was dark now, with blinking lights crawling about the road like fireflies who had forgotten how to fly. He had lost weight. His face looked thinner, not gaunt yet but getting there soon. His hair was unkempt, and he had not shaved in weeks. His clothes too were crumpled up and thinking back he realised it had been a while since he had done any laundry at all.

'Fine,' Aryan sighed, realising that Akshay was right, and he was being ridiculous, 'But I can't go anywhere looking like this.'

'That's my boy. Who said you are going anywhere looking like this? The party's at eight. We have some time. Get up. We got a lot of work to do.'

'What party?'

'Little by little through patience, the mind will become stilled in the Self.' Akshay said with a smirk.

'What is that? *The Bible*.'

'Urgh. Philistines. *The Bhagavad Gita,* my friend. Now get up. We got a lot of karma to do, and apologies to Shri Krishna, I am gonna get this city the finest fruits of it with your hot piece of ass.'

Aryan rolled his eyes in response.

They stopped at Aryan's place to pick up his last clean

shirt. They then hit a salon to get him cleaned up. Aryan complained loudly that he felt like a dog, being dragged to the groomers, but was secretly thankful for Akshay breaking him out. Left to his own devices, who knew how long he would have moped around.

They entered the party at around nine. It had already warmed up and people were dancing and drinking and in general having what passes off for a good time for the current generation.

'Do I even know anyone here?' Aryan said loudly, trying to get himself heard over the music.

'No. Neither do I. Friend of a friend of a friend. Of a friend. I think. I am not even sure.' Akshay replied, looking hungrily at a girl on the other side of the room who had caught his eye.

'Should we even be here?'

'Yes. I have a message with this place's address. And if anyone asks, you are a friend of Raj's. Every party has a Raj. Lord bless moms who were pregnant when DDLJ came out,' Akshay offered unhelpfully, his eyes still stuck to the girl, who had noticed him and was making eye contact with enough frequency to encourage him.

'So, erm, yeah. Get a drink. Hang around. Talk to people. Whatever. I gotta go, bye,' Akshay called out over his shoulder, as he made his way to the other side of the room leaving Aryan to his own devices.

Aryan looked around for a second. The party was like any other house party in the country, that Aryan could recall from something that felt like another life. A table on one side of the hall which would have drooped under the weight of the bottles if they all had not been half empty. The yellow lights had been switched out for flashing, coloured lamps that made him giddy. The same generic music with thumping beats and bare minimum nursery rhyme like lyrics, the lowest common denominator, was blasting out the speakers. Lord forbid, if someone played any music with some character whatsoever. There were maybe thirty or so people at the party, nearly everyone with a glass in one hand, and many with cigarettes or joints burning innocuously in the other.

Aryan walked slowly to the bar and started mixing himself a scotch with water and ice. The alcohol was cheap, cheaper than he was used to. His first swig took him back to his college days when this was all he could afford and loved it anyway. Money had maybe ruined getting drunk for him. He was now too concerned with not disrespecting the fine whiskey to get sloshed and dance like a madman. He took his glass and stood in one corner of the room, trying not to get noticed. He saw Akshay flirting generously with the girl in the other corner of the room. He smiled to himself. Once upon a time, he would have beat him to it. Now, he did not feel like it. Or cared.

'Hi. Enjoying yourself?'

Aryan turned to see a short girl, rather cute, looking up at him. She was dressed in a black off shoulder top and distressed denim shorts, paired with cheap earrings bought at Connaught Place after haggling with the shopkeeper for hours, and belle flats. She had hair reaching her shoulder which was dyed a soft burgundy and framed her face well.

'Er, yeah. Is this your place?'

'Yes. I don't think we have met. Hi. I am Sneha. Sneha Khanna.'

'Aryan. Aryan Sinha. Great party.'

'Thanks. So, who are you here with?'

'Er, actually. I am not sure. I came with a friend, who was invited by a friend and well, you know, after a while I stopped questioning it. I just wanted to get him off my back.'

Sneha laughed, throwing her head back. The laugh of a person who liked laughing and liked hearing herself laugh.

'Not a party person?'

'Erm, I don't know. I used to be. I am not sure anymore.'

'Hmm. I know. Happens,' Sneha offered with a solemn nod and took a deep swig from her glass.

'What are you drinking?' Aryan asked, more out of politeness than anything else.

'Vodka and cranberry. I am a basic bitch. Deal with it!' Sneha grinned at him, 'What about you?'

'Scotch on the rocks. Basic bro, reporting for duty!' Aryan did a mock salute and made Sneha laugh. She returned the salute and turned to stand beside him, leaning on the wall.

'Please, don't let me keep you. I am sure you must have your host duties.'

'No. I am tired. And I am done. So done.'

'Wait, didn't you throw this party?' Aryan asked, raising his eyebrows.

'Yeah. I did. But it's just something that I do. Every weekend. It has sort of become this ritual and I don't want to break it, so this keeps going on. But sometimes you feel like being alone.'

'Huh! What happened?'

'Life. Life happened.'

Aryan nodded and looked into his drink. Great! Another one of those.

'I know what you are thinking,' Sneha said before Aryan could say anything.

'You do?'

'You bet. You are thinking, "Great! Another one of those emo girls who had like one breakup and now has to mask that pain and pretend her life is so broken. Basically go Gatsby on this world in her melodrama." I get that a lot.'

'What? No! What made you think that?' Aryan said, not meeting her gaze.

'Oh please. I wasn't born yesterday.'

They stood side by side for a few minutes in silence, steadily getting more awkward.

'Can I ask you something?' Sneha said.

'Yeah, sure.'

'I know it's random, but do you ever think about death?'

'I'm sorry?'

'Yeah. Like, we are here. And one day we will not be anymore. And no one knows what happens then. So, shouldn't we make the most of the time that we do have? Instead of, you know, putting it off for another time. Which may never come. Like, on the way back you could get hit by a car and die. Or anything could happen. What happens then? All plans will lie splattered on the road. You would have died without really living.'

'Oh...kay.'

'Oh God! I am so stupid. I am rambling again. Come on. You are dry. Let's get you another drink.' Sneha spoke, suddenly her voice was a lot more present, as if in the last few minutes, she was another person.

Aryan gestured with her hand for her to lead the way and slowly shook his head once he was behind her. He looked around for Akshay, but he was nowhere to be seen. Neither was the girl. Well, at least someone was having a good time at the party!

He followed Sneha to the bar and refilled their drinks. She broke off to go to a group of girls dancing in the middle of the room. A resounding 'Woo!' confirmed to Aryan that the meeting had been successful. He walked around the room, looking for a place to sit, trying not to bump into half-drunk people. He stopped in front of a wooden showcase, with glass panes. Inside were all sorts of things you would be hard pressed to find in any dwelling in the country with only male inhabitants—souvenirs, pictures in pretty frames, candles, curios.

He started scanning the pictures to pass his time. Akshay wasn't picking up his phone. Clearly, he had found better uses for his hands. The pictures painted a life that was interesting but certainly not unique. Sneha went to hill stations, to the beach, hung out with her friends at clubs, and had a few pictures with a dog. Aryan stood there transfixed. It was like looking into the past, from when people had cameras with a physical film reel, that was developed, and a lot of the pictures were blurry. But then you took the best ones and framed them, or put them into an album with plastic covers, laminating a sliver of time. Now with Instagram, and the fifty million retakes, and everything existing and not existing at the same time, all the romanticism of pictures was lost. But here they were—pictures in frames. Something you could look at without the blue, sterile light of a screen. Something you could hold on to, something you could give away.

Something about one of the pictures caught his eye and leaned forward. It was nothing extraordinary. Sneha standing cheek-to-cheek with another girl, a glass in her hand. It was probably taken at a club. He peered in closely and suddenly it clicked why the picture had caught his eye.

He ran to where Sneha was, grabbed her by the hand and pulled her out.

'You will not believe it, but I have been looking for you for so long!'

'What? What are you talking about?'

'Yes. I need a favour from you. I know someone you know. I need her number.'

'What?'

'Yeah. I know it sounds crazy, but I ran into her in Manali a month ago. We hung out and talked all night and decided to meet once we were back in Delhi. But the number she gave me wasn't working.'

'Wait. Who are you talking about?'

'Rashmi. Rashmi Agarwal. That's her in the picture there, right?'

Sneha's face drained of colour immediately, as if she had seen a ghost.

'Rashmi Agarwal has been dead for a year.'

Chapter 4

Aryan shifted uncomfortably in his seat, more because of the situation he was in than the lumpy cushion. The room was decorated modestly, with all the declarations of it being a middle-class household. The remote control was covered in plastic, there was a crocheted cover over every piece of electrical equipment in the house, topped with a small clay figurine that you bought at the China market. Aryan scanned the room for pictures but there were very few on the walls, and none of Rashmi. Maybe they had taken them off after she passed away. He had no way of telling. There wasn't even the customary picture with garlands on it that were put up in all Indian households in the memory of those who pass away. Aryan found that highly irregular but did not dare ask about it. Different people dealt with death differently. He sipped the tea and winced; it did not have any sugar. Diabetics, he decided.

It had not taken a lot to convince Sneha to take him to Rashmi's parents. Her own guilt over Rashmi's death, combined with the optimism of getting a new lead had made her a very willing collaborator. The Agarwals, Deepak and Suman, lived in a modest apartment on the edge of Delhi, in Noida. Suman Agarwal was dressed in a sober sari when Aryan and Sneha arrived and welcomed them politely. They made small talk, Aryan suspected Sneha had not told them why Aryan wanted to meet them, maybe to soften the blow and not make them anxious beforehand. Once the tea was over, all of them, Aryan, Sneha and the Agarwals, sat in a tense silence, unsure of how to begin.

'I am sure you must be wondering why I have come to meet you. Actually, I had a very strange experience and I wanted to talk to you about it,' Aryan spoke once it was clear he could not put it off anymore. He took a deep breath and began.

'A month or so ago, I was in Manali with some friends. And there, I met someone claiming to be Rashmi.'

Suman clapped her hand to her mouth and looked at Aryan in shock. Deepak's lips thinned and he stared hard at Aryan, waiting for him to continue.

'Have you seen any suspicious activity on her credit card. Or a phone bill? Or something of that sort? Because we think it's a case of stolen identity and someone is pretending to be Rashmi.'

'Is this a joke?' Deepak said loudly.

'No Uncle. I thought so too when he bumped into me. But he is telling the truth. He had her phone number and everything,' Sneha quickly intervened.

Deepak still stared at Aryan, not entirely sold on his story.

'Well, no. We cancelled all her cards. Her number has been out of use. We had a few fixed deposits in her name. For her marr...anyway. We broke those too. Whoever it was, they are not swindling anyone for money using our daughter's name.'

'Can I see her phone?'

'We never found it. It was not there with...' Deepak trailed off again, his voice breaking.

'But why would anyone be doing it?' Suman said, panic rising in her voice.

'We don't know Aunty. We are trying to figure that out ourselves.' Sneha offered kindly.

'Let's go to the Police.' Suman looked at Deepak.

'AND WHAT GOOD WILL THAT BE?' Deepak burst out, leaving both Aryan and Sneha stunned, 'We run there every month. Have they ever lifted a finger to help us get some closure? All they care about is closing the file. Bloody bastards, all of them.'

Suman fell silent, more out of the humiliation than anything else.

'I completely understand, Uncle. We are not sure what is happening either.'

'Where did you meet this person?' Deepak asked gruffly.

'In Manali. A little outside the town. We spent the nig... evening roaming around the city. She gave me her number.'

'I checked the number. It was correct. That was the number Rashmi used,' Sneha chimed in.

'What did she look like?' Deepak shot back.

'Well, I don't have a picture, but very similar to Rashmi. Here. This was a portrait I drew of her,' Aryan pulled out a slightly crumpled napkin from his shirt pocket and handed it. Suman reached hungrily for it. Aryan felt sad as he cast another look at the napkin. He had saved it, planning to give it to Rashmi when he met her once they were back in Delhi.

'She looks a lot like Rashmi. Don't you think?'

Deepak looked at it briefly and turned away.

'It's a drawing. What good will that be?'

'No. Look at it! It is a good drawing. It really looks like our Rashmi.' Suman continued to look lovingly at the napkin.

'Our Rashmi is dead!' Deepak said once again, much softer this time, his eyes to the floor.

Suman's eyes welled up when she heard this. Sneha quickly got up from beside Aryan and rushed to sit beside her, holding her hand and stroking it gently. Deepak looked at them with a pained expression.

'Look, I appreciate you telling us this. We will inform the police about it the next time we go to Manali. But other than that, I don't know how else we can help you.'

'Well, why don't you take a look around?' Suman jumped in before Deepak could dismiss Aryan and Sneha.

Deepak's eyes narrowed as he glared at Suman fiercely, shaking his head.

'What? The poor boy has been asking so much. It is the least we can do. Come with me.' Suman rose, gesturing the door that led inwards, deeper into the house.

'FINE! Take him to Rashmi's room. I don't care,' Deepak said loudly.

Aryan looked at Sneha who nodded. He rose from his seat and walked towards Suman with small, unsure steps. She lifted the curtain on the door to let him in.

The living room led into a hall, which was connected to a kitchen, a bathroom and two rooms on the far end. The hall was furnished modestly, with an engineered wood dining table and chairs, a fridge and an inverter cabinet. There were pictures of deities and cheap, dusty souvenirs that middle class people bought anytime they went anywhere hanging on the wall permanently.

She unlocked the room and opened the door for Aryan. He swayed on his toes on the edge of the room, unsure if he wanted to go in but then let himself fall forward. The first thing he saw was a large picture of Rashmi hanging on the opposite wall.

His heartbeat quickened. He had not made a mistake. It was Rashmi he had seen that day. There was no doubt about it. He felt the blood draining from his face and rushing away to leave him cold and clammy. His head swam and he had to grab the door frame to remain standing. He extended a step gingerly into the room and the second his feet touched the floor, his mind flooded with images of that night. Him and Rashmi walking up the hill. Talking in the cafe, sipping coffee. Walking around the city square. He unsteadily walked in and sat down on the chair in front of the worktable set overlooking the window that got the beautiful view of another brick wall.

There was another picture of Rashmi's right in front of his face, framed and put with care in front of a vase of plastic flowers. He gazed at the picture, Rashmi's innocent, beautiful face staring back at him, frozen in time.

'Are you ok? You are looking a little pale.' Suman asked, putting a hand on his shoulder, looking concerned.

'What? No, yes. I am fine. Just felt a bit dizzy.'

'It's ok.'

She waited for a few seconds and then said, 'Well, look around. Everything is how she left it. We haven't touched anything.'

Suman quickly turned, her eyes welling up again and left Aryan alone in the room.

Aryan looked around. The room was in stark contrast to the rest of the house. It was tastefully decorated with decals, posters and fairy lights. There was a glass showcase on one wall which was full of little trinkets. A wooden cupboard was kept beside the door with a full-length mirror on one door. There was a beanbag kept in a corner, right under a small bookshelf with a dozen or so books neatly stacked on it.

Aryan moved around the room, looking over the bookshelf, not sure of what he was looking for. He felt stupid wandering around the room not knowing what he was supposed to do. He touched the knob of the drawer of the work desk but pulled away his hand, not wanting to invade her privacy—kind of invalidating the whole idea of an investigation.

He stood at the door, throwing one last look at the room,

chiding himself for coming here. He had no idea what he was doing and all he had managed to do was bring up old wounds for a couple who had lost their only daughter and made a fool of himself.

Just as he turned to leave the room, he heard a rustling behind him. He turned to see an old photo fluttering down to the ground. He reached out and caught it midair and looked up to see where it had fallen from, or how. He could not see anything. It was as if the photo had just materialised from thin air. He stood there confused for a second, trying to figure out how the picture got there.

It must have fallen from the top of the shelves or something, he reasoned with himself and looked at the picture. It was a polaroid photograph—one of those retro ones where the picture developed immediately. It was taken outside a club. It was Rashmi with a man who had a shaved head and a muscular body. He was dressed in a black t-shirt. There was something written on the shirt and Aryan peered closely to read what it said.

It was a club logo, 'Anywhere.' Something flashed in his head almost immediately.

Aryan stumbled out, banging his shoulder out into the door frame and walked back as quickly as he could to the living room.

'Sneha, I need to talk to you,' he spat out, the urgency was clear in his voice.

'Sure,' Sneha rose from her seat unsure of what it was all about.

Aryan pulled her into Rashmi's old room and Sneha stuttered to a halt at the door. She knew the room well. She had spent many afternoons there after school, many sleepovers talking about everything that had happened that day.

'Do you know who this is?' Aryan thrust the photo at her.

'No,' Sneha looked at the picture closely and shook her head.

'Think hard.'

'I really don't know. Rashmi had a lot of friends,' Sneha replied with a shrug.

'Do you know a guy named Roy?'

'I don't think so. How do you know that?'

'Rashmi had mentioned…'

'The girl you met,' Sneha corrected her fiercely.

'Right, that. Well, she had mentioned she had a friend named Roy who worked in Hauz Khas Village as a bartender. This picture looks like it was taken in front of a club. It is worth checking out.'

'Are you sure?'

'No. But why would she have a picture of this guy in her room? If they were so close, you would certainly know about him. If you don't, maybe he knows something more.'

'Who is that?' Deepak's voice rang out behind them, and they both turned around in surprise, as if caught doing something illegal.

'Do you know him?' Aryan quickly regained his wits and showed the picture to Deepak.

'No. I don't know. Who is he?' He returned the picture to Aryan after taking a long look.

'A bartender named Roy. I think. Sneha doesn't know him, but I remember whoever I met in the mountains mentioned someone who matches the description. And here is a picture of them together.'

'Where did you find it? We have never seen this,' Deepak asked Aryan.

'It fell down. From the top of the shelf, I think. I am not sure.'

'Is that so?' Deepak peered at Aryan suspiciously. Aryan felt uncomfortable under his gaze, as if he was being x-rayed.

'I think we should go talk to him,' Aryan said, his voice determined.

'Ok. I will come with you,' Deepak replied.

'What?'

'Yes. I am coming with you. I need to know how he was connected to Rashmi.'

'It's fine, Uncle. I can take care of it.'

'It is about my daughter. I am coming with you,' Deepak glared at Aryan, who immediately wilted under his gaze.

Chapter 5

The next evening Aryan, Akshay and Deepak walked up to the gate of 'Anywhere', paid their cover charge and went in, all the time drawing looks from the people around as the oddest pair—a couple of young man and a middle-aged uncle. Some of them wondered if they were spoiled brats who had brought their father to a nightclub to fight their battles. Others wondered if Deepak was a lawyer and was looking to sue the club on Aryan and Akshay's behalf.

They made their way to the crowded bar and saw Roy hard at work, mixing drinks and flirting with attractive women. They hung back in the shadows, making sure he did not see them until they had him cornered. The boys nursed warming beers to justify occupying a booth, Deepak smoked a packet of cigarettes he had carried with him.

'You want one?' Deepak offered. Aryan looked at the cigarettes, shrugged and took one.

'What happened that day? When you met that person?'

Aryan took a drag, held it in to calm his nerves before answering. He did not want to let slip that he had seen Rashmi that day in front of Deepak. It might upset him.

'So, it was the last day of our trip. We were supposed to take the bus back to Delhi that evening. I went for a stroll and ended up a little outside the main city. There was a small brook down the side of the road. I went down and there I saw a girl stumbling on the slope back to the road. I ran to help her. We climbed back up together. We then walked back to the city. I felt like we had a connection, so we decided to skip our travel plans and roamed around the city the entire night, just talking. She then left around 3.30 am in the night to go back to her friends and I never saw her again.'

'And she told you her name was Rashmi Agarwal?' questioned Deepak.

'Yes. Gave me her number too. When I met Sneha at the party by accident, I showed her the number. It was the number Rashmi used. She even told me a lot of other things about herself that Sneha also verified.'

'I don't understand it even now. Why would anyone do that?'

'What had happened? You know, last year?' Akshay asked gingerly, very uncomfortable with the mess he was in, but strong in his solidarity with Aryan.

Deepak's face hardened and he took another deep drag of the cigarette before answering.

'Rashmi was supposed to return that evening. But early in the morning we got a call from Sneha. She told us that Rashmi had not returned and they were looking for her. We set out that evening and reached Manali the next morning. We looked for her for a week. Even after Sneha and her friends left, we stayed back, asking around every shop, every cafe in the city. We got the police to look for her in the forests surrounding the city, thinking maybe there was an accident, she slipped, and fell.'

Aryan heard silently, noting everything down in his mind.

'A lot of our family came down to help as well. We looked for her for over a month. Plastering the area with posters and *Missing ads.* There were a lot of calls but most of it was useless. When we went to cross check on them, it was always I think I saw someone who looked like her. When nothing panned out, we came back to Delhi, but kept in constant touch with the local police.'

He stopped to put out his cigarette and pulled out another one. Aryan had barely had a few drags and his head was already spinning. He put out his cigarette and took another swig of the beer to soothe his throat protesting the smoke.

'We waited, visited every month, but there was nothing. Then one day, two months after we returned, we got a call from the police department that they had found a body in another district that they suspected was Rashmi's. We immediately rushed back. The body was badly decayed. It was too far gone for any sort of forensics, locally at least. Rashmi's mother identified a small birthmark that had been on her back. We wanted them to investigate further but they had already lost interest. The body had been found and that was the end of everything for them. They wanted to close the file, but we pulled some strings to make sure that they would at least keep looking. But that was all only to keep us out of their hair. They barely lifted a finger after that,' Deepak ended bitterly.

'I know this must be very difficult for you,' Aryan offered kindly, emboldened by the beer.

Deepak looked at him in surprise. He then gathered himself and simply nodded.

'Where did you do the final rites? If you don't mind me asking?'

'In Shimla they had an electric crematorium there. The body was too far gone for the customary last rites. We spread the ashes in Haridwar,' Deepak said coldly, his eyes flickering to the bar.

'I think we can go now. It's getting empty,' Deepak rose suddenly from his seat and started towards the bar. Aryan quickly chugged the last of the beer and followed him. Akshay hesitated but followed, nevertheless.

Roy was bald, like really bald, Aryan thought to himself. His head was so closely shaved that Aryan could not even tell the natural colour of his hair, or whether he had male pattern baldness. He was a short, stocky, but hulking dude, with biceps easily the size of Akshay's thighs. He was dressed in a similar black t-shirt with apparently some witty one liner about alcohol on the back that Aryan did not care about and was leaning closely to a drunk girl dressed in a sparkly mini skirt.

They got close to him and noticed him flirting unabashedly with the girl, his fingers tracing the side of her body. Aryan knew all about what flirts do, but there was something sleazy about the way Roy was doing it. Lingering on the side of her breast a second too long, his thumb wandered over the shiny fabric of her dress. He could tell that the girl was too drunk to know what was going on and was practically propped up against Roy to stay in her stool. It made him very uncomfortable, just watching. Roy had meanwhile abandoned the pretence of being delicate and was groping the girl's butt, ignoring her attempts to push his hand away.

'Are you Roy?' Deepak said menacingly the second they reached the bar. Akshay stood close behind as the world's most pointless backup in case things went south.

'That depends, who is asking?' Roy turned towards them. He moved away from the girl, slowly backing away. Questions like these often ended up into bullets in bars like these.

'I am asking. Did you know Rashmi?'

'Rashmi?'

'Rashmi Agarwal. Yes. Did you know her?' Aryan jumped in, eager to diffuse the tension.

'I don't know anyone by that name.' Roy cut him short, his lips thinning now.

'Really? Because she mentioned you. She said you are into regional food and showed her a Tibetan cafe in Manali.'

'I have no idea who you are talking about. Please leave,' Roy shot back angrily. The girl was now slumped over the bar, completely forgotten.

'Are you sure? I mean…'

'Well, then how do you explain this?' Deepak cut Aryan off mid-sentence and slapped his palm on the bar, loud enough for the couple of people around to jump away. When he moved it away, there was the polaroid on the counter.

Roy's eyes moved to the picture and for a second, Aryan

thought he saw absolute terror on his face. But he slowly moved towards them. He turned the picture around and looked at it.

'May I?' He asked Deepak. He nodded.

Roy picked up the picture slowly to his eyes and looked at it carefully. He turned to the three guys standing in front of him, trying to look menacing. Then, in a sudden movement, he tore up the picture into little bits and threw it in the dustbin.

'SECURITY! Get these drunkards out of my face. And you, if I catch you skulking around here ever again, I will break your legs. Get out!'

Stunned, they were unable to move until the bouncers came up to them and started pulling them by the arm. As soon as they were touched, however, Deepak burst out and started yelling at Roy at the top of his lungs, calling him all sorts of names and threatening every member of his family with colourful abuses. Aryan and Akshay grabbed his arm. They knew that they were in a dicey situation and whatever they could do tomorrow, they were in imminent danger of getting roughed up right now and it was best they left quietly without creating a scene. The bouncers half dragged, half carried them out of the club and threw out on the street through the backdoor.

Aryan sat up, nursing his elbow. He had cut his lip, and it was bleeding. He turned around to see Akshay, who nodded that he was okay. Deepak still raging, shaking his fist and hurling swear words that would have made a Gurgaon auto driver blush.

'Calm down, Uncle,' Aryan spoke gently, trying to quiet Deepak down.

'That bastard. That brothel born son of a whore. Who the fuck does he think he is? Tearing up my photo, I will tear him a fucking new one.'

'Relax Uncle, relax. We can't do anything right now. We will come back with the police tomorrow.'

'You bet your ass we will.'

'Yes. Let's get you home. We will think about this later,' Akshay offered gently.

Deepak was still fuming but at least his temper was milder now. He sat there breathing heavily and then heaved his heavy frame off the road. He limped towards the main road, leading away from the village, one hand over Aryan's shoulder for support.

'Did you notice something?' Deepak said once they were out of the village and were on the main road.

'What?'

'He recognised Rashmi from the picture. His eyes grew wide, and his face turned pale. He knows something,' Deepak said softly, his eyes fixed on the road ahead.

Chapter 6

Aryan shifted in his seat, going over the story in his head. He had gone through multiple iterations of what he wanted to say to the police about the whole situation but found himself at a dead end every time in his mind. Deepak sat beside him, looking squarely into the distance, his jaw set in stone.

'This is a waste of time,' Deepak shot out after a long period of silence.

'Let us try once,' Aryan pleaded.

'You think we have not tried all of this? We dug up every contact we had, went to every police station between here and Manali. Nothing happened. There were all excuses. Sometimes it was out of their jurisdiction. Others, the case has a different office in-charge. It felt like no one cared, from top to bottom,' Deepak spoke through gritted teeth.

Aryan wasn't sure how to reply. He found it very difficult to believe that no one from the system would help. Maybe Deepak's temper had gotten in the way, he reasoned with himself. Well, he was a calm, collected person. He was not going to make the same mistake. They sat in silence, waiting to be called into the chamber of the SHO at the Hauz Khas Police Station.

The police station somehow provided a strange contrast with itself. It was teeming with people who looked more like the cast of a strange, avant-garde play than living, breathing people. Some looked like drug peddlers, others were dressed to the nines, and Aryan was not sure which was which. A group of youngsters was slumped in the corner on a bench, clearly fresh off a night in the village, probably waiting for their parents to come pick them up. Knowing the place, Aryan was sure they would not have the privilege. The best any of them were going to manage was a driver, or maybe a lawyer. Aryan thought to himself about how he would have felt in their place, relieved that he would be spared the wrath of his parents or crushed that no one cared.

A door swung open from one corner of the station, and all eyes immediately looked up hopefully. A constable wiggled his finger at Aryan and walked back in without a word. Aryan rushed to his feet and waited for Deepak to get to his feet.

They walked into the room, following the constable and saw a tall, slightly balding man behind a large wooden table, staring at a file. The pyramid shaped plaque on the desk proclaimed it belonged to one inspector Kamal Pandey. The shiny obsidian name tag on his uniform however contradicted the plaque and named the police man as sub inspector Dinesh Yadav. Without looking up from the file, Dinesh gestured at Aryan and Deepak to sit down.

'Yes. Tell me,' Dinesh spoke after a couple of minutes, still looking into the file and occasionally scribbling something on it.

'Sir, we have to make a complaint about an incident yesterday,' Aryan offered, trying to sound more confident than he felt.

'Ok. What happened?'

'This is Deepak ji. Deepak Agarwal. His daughter died last year under suspicious circumstances.'

Dinesh looked up for the first time from his file. His eyes were small, with hints of crow's feet around them. He was in his late thirties, maybe even early forties. Aryan wasn't sure how to gauge the competence of an inspector in his forties, he did not know enough the police ranks and hierarchies to adjust how he was going to talk to the sub inspector.

'Ok?'

'A complaint was filed in Manali, where the incident had happened. The investigation had been closed after the body was found and the whole thing was ruled as an accident. But we have reason to believe that it was not an accident and there was foul play.'

Aryan could see Dinesh's shoulders droop again as he returned to his file.

'Why are you coming here then? This is Delhi, the case happened in Shimla.'

'Manali.'

'Shimla, Manali, whatever. It was not Delhi. It is out of our jurisdiction.'

Deepak started to get up, but Aryan held his hand and pulled him back down.

'Yes sir, I understand,' Aryan spoke in a slow, measured tone, 'However, there is someone who we think is connected to the incident and he lives here in Hauz Khas Village. We met him yesterday and had an altercation with him.'

'So, you had a fight with someone?' Dinesh asked, his eyes still glued to the file.

'Yes.'

'Then say that. What is this cock and bull story about a death and all? I see fifty cases like this a day, people trying to make things more serious than they are.'

'Sir…'

'Uncle you are old. You are mature. What are you doing here with these kids?' Dinesh looked at Deepak and said with irritation. Deepak did not reply.

'Anyway, what happened?' Dinesh asked Aryan, finally putting his file to a side.

'We went to meet this person yesterday. His name is Roy. We found a picture of him with Rashmi, the deceased. He tore up the picture and got us thrown out of the club.'

'Ok. What do you want me to do now?'

'Sir? He tore up an important piece of evidence…' Aryan started incredulously.

'You think this is a court or what? Important evidence? If it was so important, why didn't you go to the police first? You guys go around, trying to be smart, and then come crying to us afterwards.'

Aryan gripped the handle of his chair, trying to calm himself down. Maybe Deepak was right, after all. It was not his fault. He had not picked a fight with the police in his hurt and righteous temper. It did look like no one wanted to listen.

'Well, we are coming now,' Aryan said softly.

'Oh! Thank you so much! We are much obliged,' Dinesh replied sarcastically, 'Do you have his number?'

'Roy's? No.'

'Any address? Where does he live?'

'He works at 'Anywhere'. It's this club in Hauz Khas Village.'

'Anywhere'. There were reports of disturbance there yesterday night. Was it you?'

'Sir?' Aryan was unsure how to reply.

'Yes. Good thing you showed up yourself. They did not have anything other than a vague description. It's a 324 case. Non bailable, three years.'

Aryan felt the blood draining from his body. He had no idea it was going to turn into this. He had come in looking for help, and here he was getting booked himself, for a crime that he did not commit.

'What are you saying, sir? I did not do anything.'

'Tell that to the magistrate. We have a complaint against you. We are arresting you based on that FIR. Tell whatever you want to the magistrate,' Dinesh replied, his eyes gleaming in sadistic pleasure.

'Can I see a copy of the FIR?' Deepak spoke before Dinesh could make a move towards the bell calling in his constable.

'What?'

'Yes. You received a complaint. There must be a copy of the FIR, right?'

'I don't need to show it to you,' Dinesh replied haughtily.

'You do. You are arresting someone and taking them in front of the magistrate without a chargesheet, or an arrest warrant?'

'Are you a lawyer?'

'Yes. Yes, I am. And what else did you say—324? Where is the weapon? Have you found anything on the suspect? Search him right now. If you don't find anything, how are you charging him with 324? Do you think we are all idiots?'

'Listen…'

'No. You listen,' Deepak's voice was now steel cold, 'I knew what was going to happen, but the kid did not listen to me. I lost my daughter and through all of it, none of you did anything. I have made peace with it, but don't think for a second, I have let go of it. Come on Aryan, we are leaving.'

'Just wait a minute,' Dinesh started, a bit louder.

'No. We are leaving. If you really have an arrest warrant, you will have the address, and the chargesheet. Come and arrest him. But I will not sit here and let you harass this child who was just looking to get some help from you.'

Deepak got up, turned on his heels and walked out of the room. Aryan scrambled to his feet and followed quickly. He did not want to give the sub-inspector an opportunity to change his mind and cause further problems. They walked briskly to the car and Aryan gunned it forward, not slowing down till they had reached the Delhi-Noida border.

He pulled the car into the parking lot of Deepak's house and sat there holding the steering so tightly, his knuckles turned white.

'I know how these bastards think and work,' Deepak offered helpfully after some time.

'They tried to pin it on me,' Aryan spoke through gritted teeth.

'Just trying to make a quick buck. I told you. There is no point in going to them.'

'You were right. I should have listened to you.'

'It's ok. Despite every occasion, every time I walk in, I do have some hope. It's not your fault.'

'So, what do we do next?' Aryan asked.

'I don't know. But whatever it is that we do, it's just us. We cannot depend on the police. They are useless.'

Aryan nodded and sat there. Deepak waited for a few seconds, wondering if he should say something but then decided against it finally. He got out of the car and walked slowly towards the elevator. Aryan backed the car out and drove out of the apartment complex.

For the first time in months, he was feeling utterly helpless and alone.

Chapter 7

'He is exiting the elevator. Are you sure we want to do this? It's still not too late,' Deepak spoke softly into his phone, cupping the mouthpiece with his hand, crouched behind a car in the underground parking lot of the mall.

'Yes. No point turning back now. He is alone, we might never get another chance like this to get answers from him,' Aryan spoke in a low growl, staring at the approaching figure of Roy.

Aryan needed answers and he had run out of options. The police clearly was not interested in anything. He had tried it all. The police in Manali weren't keen on opening a closed case based on a hunch, while the police in Delhi refused because the case was out of their jurisdiction. He had spent nearly a month bobbing back and forth between Manali and Delhi, police stations, and administrative officers he had managed to get in touch with. But at the end, one thing became very clear to him—he was on his own.

Aryan looked at his watch—anytime now. He had been studying Roy's movements for weeks. He had even cornered

Roy twice, but he had managed to slip away every time. Roy had made it crystal clear that he was going to be infuriatingly unhelpful. The more he ran away from answering their questions, the more suspicious Aryan got.

Always protected by his bouncers, surrounded by people, Roy had started to piss Aryan off with his stubbornness. Aryan needed him alone. Away from the safety of the crowd.

Aryan ran over the plan in his head. He was prepared for every eventuality, every backup, backed up with two more backups, like a deranged fractal of possibilities. In the worst-case scenario, he could always ditch everything and run. Roy had no idea who he was. Sure, to someone on the street his plan might have sounded a little like overkill, but it was the safest way. There would be no violence, no one would get hurt, and he would find out all he needed to know. It would just be a conversation, with a little theatricality thrown in as grease for Roy's tongue.

'Ok. I will be behind his car to distract him. You creep up from behind and do your thing, Are you sure? Last chance!' Deepak said, excited despite his age.

'Of course, I am sure. Ok. He is coming. Get ready.'

'OYE! You! Baldy! You think you are so tough?' Deepak stumbled out from behind Roy's car and yelled out at him, putting on an impressive act of being drunk. Aryan had counted on Roy's overconfidence to do the rest.

Roy stiffened for a second and then started walking quickly to his car. Aryan crouched behind the pillar next to his car. He would only get one shot at this.

'Get away from the car!' Roy yelled, still a few feet away.

'OR WHAT? You young guys think you are so tough! Well, I fought in the war!'

'Get away from the car or there will be another one right here. Get out of here!' Roy yelled out, now jogging towards the car. He stopped right in front of the car, facing the windshield.

Aryan felt panic rising in his throat. He needed Roy trapped in the narrow space between the two cars for his plan to work.

'Key his car. Bang on the door! Come on! Something! I need him close to the door,' Aryan muttered, hoping the old man would be able to improvise.

Deepak without missing a beat, pulled out a key from his pocket and started tapping the rear passenger window of Roy's red SUV.

'I will tell you what war is, you bald bastard! Come here and fight like a man,' he slurred out. Roy moved quickly and grabbed Deepak's hand and twisted it.

In a flurry of motion, Deepak pulled his other hand out from behind his back and pushed on the spray nozzle hard. Mace squirted out in a thick white jet, and everything went black for Roy. Screaming out of pain, he tried to pull away, but Deepak had pinned his hand against the car with all his weight. Before he could extricate himself, he felt something creeping up behind him. He turned his face towards it, able to see only a vague outline from his half blind eyes. The figure grabbed him around the neck and Roy felt a sharp sting in his neck—60,000 volts of electricity ran through his body and Roy crumbled into a heap on the floor.

'Is he out?' Deepak asked, breathing heavily from the effort of having kept Roy pinned against the car.

'Yes. Not for too long though. Quickly, turn his head.' Aryan knelt beside him and pulled out a metal syringe from his backpack.

In one of the rehearsals, he had found out, to his surprise, that knocking people out with a whiff of chloroform was mostly silver screen bullshit. It smelled horrible and took five minutes to work. Deepak had managed to break free and run away very easily. Every time they had tried, despite his age. Aryan had been in a fix. It was Deepak who suggested the alternative. A mixture of Propofol and Midazolam, injected intravenously. Propofol was a short acting sedative knocking you out within a minute, Midazolam kept you out for roughly six hours. Enough time for them to carry out their plan.

'Give me his phone. I will leave it in his car and drive it back home.'

'Yeah. Here,' Aryan extended Roy's hand out to Deepak, 'Unlock it. It will have the address.'

'You have your burner phone?'

'Yeah. My phone is at home, in case I need an alibi. I got this sim for a thousand bucks in Nehru Place.'

'You overpaid.'

'What?' Aryan looked up, puzzled at the sudden interjection.

'Nothing. Load him in the car and get going. Don't

deviate from the plan. Go exactly where we discussed. From here on, you are on your own.'

'Yeah. I got it. He looks heavier than he is.'

And so, they parted ways. Deepak took Roy's car and phone to drive it back to his house, putting on a cap to fool the CCTV cameras. Aryan loaded Roy in his car and set off towards the location they had picked for the rest of the night.

Chapter 8

Roy slowly came to his senses. He shook his head trying to clear it. He was exiting the mall after a party. He had met a guy—old, thin, drunk man—in the parking lot. His eyes stung. His head hurt. He tried to massage it, but his hands didn't move. Slowly, as he gathered his wits, he realised his hands were tied behind his back. He was seated on a hard, wooden chair and had a smelly blindfold on his eyes and another rag stuffed in his mouth.

'Feel the breeze on your face?' a deep voice rang out from behind him, 'You are twelve storeys up. One gentle little push and you will make the pavement a nice Jackson Pollock. So, no screaming and shouting. Are we clear?'

Roy nodded fiercely.

'Don't worry. I just need a few questions answered. After that, you are free to go. I'll even give you the cab fare. But only if you don't make my life more difficult than it already is. Nod if I am clear.'

Roy nodded again. He struggled against the ropes, but they felt tightly wound around both his hands.

'Good. So now. Where is Rashmi Agarwal?' The gag was removed from Roy's mouth, and he gasped for air.

Aryan's heart felt like it would jump out his mouth. He could feel his heartbeat in his ears. It had not been easy to bring Roy's limp body up here. He had used the elevator but dragging him in and out of it had been difficult enough. The most difficult part, one that he had not anticipated at all, was propping Roy's limp body up on the chair, and tying him up. It had taken him at least 5 tries to get the knot around Roy's wrists right.

'Rashmi Agarwal? I don't know any Rashmi Agarwal.'

'Now Roy, that's your name right? We are in an under-construction building. I have pliers, and you have one, two, three...twenty nails in all. I have a hammer and nails of all sizes. I think I saw a drill lying somewhere around here too. Is this a game you want to play?' Aryan spoke in a slow, drawn-out drawl. The nervousness had subsided. He could feel the adrenaline rising now, fuelled at his anger at Roy, giving him a rush like he had never felt before.

'I swear! I swear to God I don't know anything, please let me go!'

'Answers Roy. I will ask one more time, and if I don't get anything, I have a saw. I have never tried before and I'm getting really curious how many licks it takes to get to the centre.'

'Rashmi. Rashmi Agarwal. Wait, are you the guy from that night?'

'What guy? There are others asking about her too?'

Roy felt a hand grabbing his throat and squeezing.

'Who was asking about her? Who was it?'

'I don't know. I never got his name. He came to my bar one day with a picture of her. Saw him following me around a couple of times after that.'

'What did he look like?'

'Normal, I guess. Tall. Had an old guy with him.'

'Wait here.'

Aryan walked to the other side of the floor and pretended make a phone call. He stood there and watched Roy struggle to free himself and fail. He waited a minute and then walked back up to the chair.

'Now there Roy. Be a good boy. Don't break my heart. Stop struggling. It hurts me to see you hurt yourself,' Aryan punctuated the sentence with a hard slap across Roy's face. Aryan smiled despite himself.

'Anyway. Back to the matter at hand. Where is Rashmi Agarwal?'

'Look I swear I have no idea what you are talking about. I really don't remember anything.'

'Roy. I am losing patience now. Next time I don't get an answer from you, I will break your little toe.' Aryan snarled, stamping on Roy's foot, surprised at his own tone.

'She was this girl. Met her at my bar. We dated for a couple of weeks. Then she vanished. I found out later she had died on a trip to Manali. I got scared and wiped everything clean. When that guy came looking for her, I got spooked and had him thrown out. That is it! I swear!' Roy spoke in a rush.

'That is, it?' Aryan felt himself deflating a little. Almost immediately, his disappointment was substituted by panic suddenly rising in his head. What had he done? He had abducted someone over absolutely nothing of consequence. Roy knew Rashmi no better than he did.

'I swear to God, that is it. I swear on the ashes of my dead mother.'

'Ok. I believe you. Now sit still.'

Aryan slowly walked behind Roy to knock him out again and untie him. The whole thing had been a terrible idea from the beginning, and he was starting to realise it. He had committed a crime, getting swept up in the idea that there was some big cover-up. He was feeling dizzier by the second.

As soon as he stood behind Roy, a hand flew out towards his crotch and hit him squarely in his testicles. Aryan doubled in pain and keeled over. Roy had managed to free his hands! To his horror, Aryan saw Roy standing up from the chair, and taking off his blindfold.

'I knew it was you, you bastard. I knew I recognised the voice.' Roy kicked him in the stomach. Aryan had the wind knocked out of him.

'Fucking son of a bitch. What was that whore to you anyway that you are so fucking in love with her? Jesus. If I would have known, I would have to go through all that for one lousy fuck, I would have never even touched her.' Roy knelt down beside Aryan and punched him squarely in his face, nearly dislocating his jaw.

Aryan spat out blood, every breath hurt. It felt like Roy had cracked his ribs. He tried to get up but stumbled and fell.

'Now. What were you saying? Pliers, right? Where are those damn pliers now? I'll fucking end this whole thing tonight.' Roy strutted away, but not before kicking Aryan once again right in his solar plexus. Aryan doubled over and crumpled to the ground, his knees to his chest, watching helplessly as Roy walked towards the toolbox kept on the far side of the floor.

Aryan pushed off the ground with all his might and managed to get back to his feet. Every muscle in his body screamed in protest. He violently shook his head to clear it. He quickly looked for something he could use to defend himself. There was nothing on this side. He had cleared everything when he was tying up Roy. He looked up through the half-finished ceiling for a ladder or a rope he could use, but there was nothing there either. He stumbled to a corner, holding himself up with the help of the wall.

Aryan saw what happened next in slow motion. Roy had picked up the hammer from the toolbox and was walking slowly towards him, taunting. Just as he walked under an unfinished section of the ceiling above, there was a rumble. Both looked up in instinct and a cartload of bricks fell cleanly through the gap in the unfinished ceiling on top of Roy with a crash.

Aryan stood there in shock for a second, unable to formulate a thought. He felt a chill running down his entire body that made him nauseous. He had heard a clear crack when the bricks had hit Roy. Buried under the load of the bricks now, Roy's hand was still twitching under the pile.

Aryan crawled on all fours to the spot to check if Roy still had a pulse. He grunted to a halt next to Roy's lifeless body and felt a presence over his head. He looked up through the hole in the ceiling.

Rashmi ever so familiar face was floating above him.

The last thing he remembered before he passed out was Rashmi gliding away from the hole and out of his sight.

Chapter 9

'He is dead,' Aryan panted out the second Deepak opened the door. He had run up the stairs because the elevator was too slow.

Deepak was in his night clothes, his hair dishevelled. But he did not have the look of a person who had just been roused from his sleep. He looked like he had barely slept at all.

'Come inside,' Deepak whispered and quickly pulled Aryan in, 'My God! What happened to your face?'

'Roy. He is dead. A cart of bricks fell on him.'

'Are you sure he is dead?' Deepak said, his breath quickening. Aryan saw a look he didn't quite understand.

'Yes. I checked his pulse. Holy shit! What are we going to do?'

'Ok. Calm down first,' Deepak handed Aryan a bottle of water and sat him down on the couch, 'Tell me exactly what happened.'

Aryan took a deep breath and narrated everything that had just happened, right up to the point where he came to himself, checked Roy's pulse and then ran out in a panic.

'Were you wearing your gloves?'

'Yes. The whole time. I remembered what you had said about fingerprints.'

'Good. You didn't leave behind anything?'

'No. I didn't carry anything other than the car keys. I even got out and cleared out the tyre tracks as you had asked me to do. I will get the tyres rotated tomorrow.'

'Ok. Don't worry about that. Were you seen? Did the construction site have anyone there? Workers, guards?'

'No one. I double checked.'

'Ok. Then in that case, if all that is true, you have nothing to worry about. There is nothing there that can lead it back to you.'

'THAT IS NOT THE POINT! I just killed someone. Oh my God! I killed someone,' Aryan screamed, hyperventilating.

'No. Look at me. No. You did not. It was an accident,' Deepak said forcefully.

'How do you know that?'

'Well…,' Deepak hesitated for a second, 'well, you told me that. A cart of bricks fell on him. You could not have done that, could you?'

'No. It fell from the floor above. I think I saw…'

'What?'

'Nothing. I blacked out. I must have been imagining things.'

'Ok. Drink some water. I need you in full control before I show you this.'

'What?'

'You need to calm down before you see it. So, just take a minute. Gather yourself, we will talk after that.'

Aryan sat there heaving, his head still buzzing from the adrenaline. He took quick, deep breaths to get his heart to slow down and pushed his thoughts away from the horrifying image of Roy's mangled, bloodied body, arms sticking at odd angles. It was not his fault. It had happened by accident. And Rashmi…

'I am ok. What did you have to show me?' Aryan spoke, his breathing slowing down, after a minute of silence.

'Take a look at this, I found this on Roy's phone.' Deepak handed Aryan his phone. Aryan was confused but took it without any questions.

The screen was black, a video pulled back to the start. He hit play and immediately a raucous laughter rang out from the feeble speakers of the phone. The camera was moving a lot, and it went on a few seconds before it settled down. It stayed unfocused on the face of a girl. Her hair was a mess, and her eyes were closed. The camera came to focus on its own after a few frames and Aryan found himself staring at Rashmi's face.

But there was something wrong with the video. She did not look ok. The camera continued to pan downwards and revealed her bare breasts. They were swinging. The camera turned to show Roy's face, revelling in the act, him flexing his biceps as if to brag about what he was doing. The camera turned back to Rashmi, who lay there, nearly motionless. Her hands lay limp on her sides. She tried to push Roy away weakly a few times, but he swatted them aside without a thought, as if it was nothing. Not an actual human being's attempt to defend herself, just a minor inconvenience in what she was meant for. It took Aryan a few seconds to realise it, but Rashmi was not in her senses. She looked pale and limp, like she was drunk. Aryan stared at the phone, wrapping his head around what he was witnessing.

The camera fell again. It was picked up again, to show Roy on top of Rashmi from the side, thrusting. There was someone holding up the camera! There was more than one person in the room. The camera turned again as another guy, clean shaven, with a hooked nose and wide forehead, stuck his tongue out at it and made crude gestures. Aryan could see bottles of Vodka in the background, one empty and the other nearly so.

Aryan's hand shook as it slowly began to dawn on him. Rashmi was drugged and Roy, and whoever this other guy was, were raping her. He quickly clicked on the scroll bar below and saw that the video went on for over twenty minutes. He looked up at Deepak, and finally understood it. His eyes had been red not because he had not slept. They were bloodshot in rage, in pain, in helplessness. Aryan handed the phone back to him.

'Keep watching. There is more,' Deepak spoke through gritted teeth.

Aryan turned his eyes back to the video, his disgust growing with every second, and his regret on Roy's death fading away. He stayed there for five minutes, treating Rashmi like a ragdoll, slapping her, choking her, degrading her in every way that he could think of. He got off after a while, with a satisfied grunt. As soon as he was done, another man came into the frame, tall, thin, hairless, naked. He pulled Rashmi's near lifeless body roughly by the ankle, plopped himself on top of her and… .

Aryan could not watch any further. The phone fell from his hands. Suddenly it started making sense to him. Why Deepak was unfazed by Roy's death. Why Aryan had seen Rashmi there, when Roy had died. She wanted revenge.

'There were three of them?'

'Yes. One of them is named Shiv. Roy calls him by name once in the video. The guy who was filming, we don't know his name. But I am sure he went and… .' Deepak broke down mid-sentence and hid his face in his hands and started crying. Suman came and sat gingerly beside him and rubbed his back.

Aryan balled his hands into fists, his nails digging into his palms till they hurt. He did not care. He closed his eyes and steeled himself to pick up the phone again.

He quickly closed the video, taking care to not look at it again. He quickly went to the video's properties and studied it carefully.

'11th April. Around seven in the evening. That was a day before she disappeared, right?'

'Yes. We got the call the next morning that she was missing.'

'So, whatever happened, these guys were involved.'

'Yes. They...they killed my daughter,' Deepak spoke through the tears streaming down his face and disappeared into Suman's arms, who hugged him tightly, crying silently herself.

'Well, let's take this to the police then. It is clear proof. I have my car downstairs.' Aryan said standing up.

'Wait a minute. Sit down,' Suman replied.

'What do you mean wait? These bastards need to be hung by their thumbs and skinned alive.' Aryan replied loudly.

'Have you forgotten one of them just died hours ago? Someone dies and the next day we show up in front of the police with his phone. How long do you think it will take them to figure out we are connected to Roy's death?' Deepak replied stone faced.

Aryan gulped. He had completely forgotten that he had seen Roy get killed by…

'What can we do then? We should immediately take this to the police. They can't pin anything to us,' Aryan continued, defiantly, still seething.

'Are you sure about that? No one saw you. No CCTV, no traffic light camera, no passers-by. Can you stake the rest of your life on that?'

'If any of those has happened, they will find me eventually. Then what is the point?'

'We don't know that. We don't even know if they will start investigating it as a murder. Or find the connection. But going to them would mean serving ourselves up to them on a plate.'

'Fine, we will sit on this then. We will go to them after a few months. Once this whole thing has died down.'

'No,' Deepak spoke suddenly and sat up straight.

'What?'

'Look. I really appreciate all that you have done for us. But this is our fight now. Leave. We never met you. You never came here. You had no idea who Rashmi was.'

'What?' Aryan was taken aback.

'Yes. It is over. End of the line. You are a young man. You have your entire life ahead of you. If it ever comes back, I killed Roy. You are done. This is over.'

'I can't,' Aryan said, looking directly into Deepak's eyes.

'Yes! Yes, you can. Get out before whatever is supposed to happen, happens. You don't need to be a part of it. You have done what you had to. We will take care of it.'

'How?'

'I don't know yet. But I will figure it out. They will pay,' Deepak said, his eyes on fire.

'I can't walk away either, Uncle.' Aryan replied.

'Don't be stubborn. What reason could you have to be a part of this mess?'

'I saw Rashmi today.'

It was Deepak and Suman's turn to be taken aback.

'What?' Suman managed to choke out, her red eyes welling up again.

'Yes. I know I sound crazy, but Rashmi killed Roy. I saw her there. Roy had got free and had beaten me to an inch of my life. It was only a matter of time till he killed me or maimed me permanently at the very least. But it was Rashmi who came to save me. She dropped those bricks on Roy from the floor above. I know it sounds crazy, but I saw her there. Looking at Roy's dead body.'

A stunned silence invaded the room. Deepak sat there, his mouth hanging open. He spluttered but could not find the words to say. It was Suman who spoke after a few moments.

'Look Aryan, you were confused. You were in so much pain. You must have been hallucinating. Rashmi is dead, how could you have seen her?'

'How could I have met her in Manali either? But I did! I don't believe in ghosts either. But I know what I saw. She was there, dressed in white. I would have laughed it off myself yesterday, but after what happened today, I finally understand. It all fits. She chose me. She wants revenge on these guys for what they did to her.'

'Listen to yourself talk. Have you lost your mind? What are you saying? That Rashmi's ghost came back to kill these guys? Just listen to yourself!' Deepak said loudly.

'I know what I saw. You can't convince me otherwise. That day in her room too. She dropped that photo. There was no wind in the room, how did the photo fall from the top shelf on its own? She has been leading me here because she has chosen me.'

Deepak hung his head in resignation. Aryan stared at them defiantly.

'Ok. Listen, it has been a long day. We have all gone through a lot. Go back home. Get some sleep. We will talk about it tomorrow. Ok?'

Aryan started to protest but then decided against it. They were right. He was charged up. He was scared and angry and confused all at the same time. Maybe all this would make sense in the morning.

'Ok,' he said softly and turned to leave.

'Just remember this Aryan. People who die, they don't come back. No matter how much we want them to,' Suman called out after him.

Aryan paused for a second, then quietly closed the door behind himself.

Chapter 10

Aryan locked the door to his room and sank to the floor. He sat there, staring blankly at the wall in front of him. He did not know what to process first. Whether he should think about how he had kidnapped and killed Roy. Or how Roy had raped, no, gang raped Rashmi. Or how Rashmi's spirit was looking for revenge and made sure Roy got what he deserved.

He peeled the clothes off himself, kicked off his shoes and carefully put it all in a large plastic bag. Deepak had told him to get rid of them, to make sure nothing remained in his house that could tie him to the murder scene. Murder scene. Aryan slowly repeated the words to himself. Was it a murder if a ghost, did it?

Ghosts, he shook his head. He was losing it. Who was going to believe that a ghost killed Roy? He had kidnapped him. He was there when Roy died. Even though he had wiped the chair clean, there were a million places he could have left his fingerprints. Even though he had worn gloves who knew what forensics were capable of. All he had planned was a shakedown, this was never supposed to be a murder. But here he was, tied to the crime scene. If the police ever found their way to him, there was no way for him to prove that he did not kill Roy. He would go to jail. Him, and not Roy and those other monsters who had raped Rashmi. She was dead. No one would prosecute a case where the victim had been dead for a year. Sure, they would take down the complaint, and pretend to investigate half-heartedly. But in the end, it would all amount to nothing. He had seen all that over the last month.

Aryan walked into the bathroom and turned on the hot water. He stood there for a quarter of an hour, scrubbing hard, in case Roy's DNA had rubbed off on him. His chest and face had turned purple where everywhere Roy had kicked him, and it made him wince every time he touched it accidentally.

He stood there scrubbing until the water got cold and then walked out of the bathroom, pulled on a pair of shorts and fell face first into his bed. He tried to close his eyes but every time he did, he saw flashes. Roy's fingers twitching as the rest of his body lay buried under bricks, Rashmi's bare breasts swinging as she tried to fight off Roy but couldn't even keep her hands up, Rashmi's pale, white face peering from the hole in the ceiling. Aryan's eyes flew open and sat up on his bed panting. He stumbled to the cupboard and found an old bottle of whiskey and poured himself a stiff drink and sat on the balcony. He sat there for hours, nursing the warming drink in his hand, taking a swig every now and then, staring blankly at the sky. Somewhere right before dawn, he finally dozed off and started dreaming,

He was back in Manali. Next to the stream where he had seen Rashmi for the first time. He was bare footed and stood ankle deep in the water. He heard a rustling of leaves from behind him. He turned and peered at it; the rustling grew louder. He cautiously walked towards the bushes and peaked through it. He saw Roy's naked body heaving. There were others surrounding him, laughing, pointing, sometimes at Roy, sometimes at Aryan.

He stepped forward and saw Rashmi under Roy. Her eyes grew alive as she saw Aryan and screamed for help. Aryan stumbled on his feet and ran towards her. But suddenly the stream around his legs started to freeze. He couldn't move his feet at all. He stood there stuck as Roy high fived the guy standing beside him and got off. For a second, Aryan's eyes met Rashmi's and she yelled, now furious rather than afraid or in pain.

'Avenge me!'

Aryan tried to move but found the ice around his feet keeping him rooted to the spot. He bent and slapped and punched the ice, making his knuckles bleed but it wouldn't give. He looked up to see that he was not in the mountains anymore. He blinked and looked around and found himself sitting in the under construction building where he had taken Roy. There was a pile of bricks right in front of him. He stood up, his feet free now. He could see a hand sticking out from under the pile of rubble, bloodied and still twitching. He ran to the pile but the more he ran the further it seemed. From the distance, he could see a white figure descending, floating down to the pile. It bent down and picked up a hammer. Aryan screamed, begging it to stop. The figure raised the hammer and brought it crashing down on the twitching hand. Again. Again. The twitching eventually stopped.

Aryan suddenly found himself moving forward. He ran to the rubble and kneeled before it. The white figure, which had stopped pounding the hand with a hammer, turned to Aryan. It was Rashmi, but her face was bloody, from the splashes of blood.

'Avenge me. Or I will.'

She then exploded like a bomb and Aryan could feel his face melting off from the heat of the blast.

His eyes flew open. It was morning. The rays of the rising sun had just hit his eyelids.

Chapter 11

Inspector Kamal Pandey took off his cap and wiped the sweat from his receding hairline. The sun was beating down on him, as it did no matter what month of the year it was in this dusty, noisy part of the city. Like a beast never satiated, the city of Delhi expanded in all directions, consuming whatever came in its way to feed its hunger. This part of the city, once on the outskirts, with nothing but farmlands and marshes, was now an upcoming suburb where upper middle-class couples bought squished together apartments to fulfil their truly middle-class aspirations.

He would have liked for the area to be cordoned off, but the state's police did not believe in such formalities. People milled about, police, workers, journalists, curious on-lookers. If there had been any footprints here, they were not usable anymore. Kamal sighed in resignation and walked to the building.

The grey building stood like a behemoth in front of him. Already built to maybe fifteen floors and showing no signs of stopping. There were blocks around in varying degrees of completion, and the tallest looked easily over thirty storeys.

He walked into the ground floor and found it teeming with people, most of them without any reason to be there.

'Sir, good morning, sir. I am Dharmendra Rathi. I am with the company working on this project. Would you come to the side please?'

Great start, Kamal thought to himself. He had to deal with these scum sucking parasites who thought that everything was for sale before he even got to the crime scene.

'Very unfortunate incident sir. Really unfortunate. But what can we do about it?' the middle-aged, potbellied man continued ingratiatingly.

Kamal grunted in response, taking in the environment. The walls were built but had several openings for easy movement of materials. That meant a lot of exits for the culprit. The floor was dusty, but he knew he had a snowball's chance in hell of getting anything usable from it. He walked towards the stairs leading up to the crime scene.

'Sir. Please sir, see if something can be worked out. If this goes to court, it will waste everyone's time. And for what? A simple accident. My employers are…'

'Will you please let me do my job?' Kamal finally yelled back, making Rathi jump back in surprise.

'Sir… .' Rathi started to speak again.

'If I hear one word from you, I don't care who your employer is, I am taking you in for obstructing an active investigation.'

Rathi fell silent and Kamal pushed him out of the way roughly and walked up to the elevator and pressed the button. Nothing happened. Power cut. Kamal cursed loudly and walked towards the stairs.

Twelve floors. Even though Kamal was in good shape for a thirty-eight-year-old man, he was not as young as he used to be. He had developed a potbelly over the last couple of years, and his regular sessions at the gym had been swapped out for making files in triplicate about every case that passed his way. He was panting by the time he reached the crime scene and had to sit down for a minute before he felt he was ready to talk to anyone.

'SI Dinesh Yadav, sir,' a young man dressed in a crisp Khaki uniform, in his mid-twenties saluted Kamal.

'What is this drama going on downstairs? Get everyone off the premises. What kind of investigation are you running here?' Kamal barked back, still catching his breath. Dinesh looked a little offended but turned and started barking orders at his constables, who immediately rushed down. The chain of screaming—the grease that keeps all institutions moving along.

'Is the forensics team here?' Kamal spoke, getting to his feet.

'Not yet, sir. We are a bit short staffed. They had to go respond to a case in Central Delhi. They will be here in another hour or so.'

Kamal scoffed in disgust. Typical. They won't give him a forensics team in time, and then, three weeks down the line, if the right people called up the right people, the SP would be after his life about why there was no progress in this case. It was the same thing every time.

'Walk me through it. What happened?'

'We got a call today morning. The construction crew found the body around five in the morning. We immediately sent a patrol car, and I came around soon after. It looks like an accident. A wheelbarrow full of bricks fell on the guy. Instant death. The body has been sent for the postmortem but it was clear he had broken his neck. Multiple compound fractures.' Dinesh parroted off with the enthusiasm of a kindergartener showing off his homework.

'Have you identified the victim?'

'Yes, sir. Rohan Yadav, twenty-seven, native of Panipat. Had a local address proof of Hauz Khas Village in his wallet. I have sent a team there to ask around in the neighbourhood.'

'Have you informed the next of kin?'

'Not yet, sir. We are trying to get hold of their contacts.'

'Why not? What about his phone?'

'There wasn't one, sir.'

'He did not have a phone?' Kamal looked back in surprise.

'No, sir. We only found his wallet with the body, a watch and a couple of rings.'

'His car. Bike. Anything?'

'No, sir. All vehicles are accounted for.'

'Were there any bottles of alcohol around? Syringes? Anything of that sort?' Kamal looked around the floor. Perfect place for junkies.

'No, sir. Nothing. The blood work is pending, but that will tell us if he was drunk.'

'He wasn't.'

'Sir?'

'He wasn't drunk. If he was, where are the bottles? And if someone removed the bottles, then it is not an accident.'

'Sir, I mean...are you sure?' Dinesh offered meekly.

'What is a Hauz Khas village guy doing in Vaishali in the middle of the night, without his cell phone, without a car? How did he even get here? The closest metro station is kilometres away. You can't get an auto at that time of the night here. Even if you can, why would he be here? He is not drinking or doing drugs. Even if he was, why here? Why not his own place? He lives in the fucking village. That place has more drugs than we know about. It doesn't add up. It's not an accident, it's a murder.'

Dinesh fell silent and nodded. He did not have the guts to contradict his senior. Not that he wanted to either. Everything Kamal had said made sense and confirmed his own hunches. There was a reason Kamal was the go-to guy for murders in the NCR area.

'But why murder sir? Why not shoot the guy? Or poison him? Or hell, even throw him off the building.'

'Now, you are asking the right questions,' Kamal smiled. Dinesh looked pleased with himself.

'I don't know yet,' Kamal continued, 'maybe someone wanted to pass it off as an accident but did not think it through properly. Lots of rookie mistakes. Or maybe, it was an accident, but there were other people here, who then turned tail and ran instead of calling for help. We don't have any witnesses, but I bet there was more than one person here.

Either way, something has gone down here last night, and we need to figure out what.'

'Right, sir,' Dinesh nodded earnestly.

'Get me the postmortem report. And call me the second the forensics team gets here. I want to talk to them before they start turning this place upside down. Also, get me his phone records. I will go talk to the neighbours and see if they know anything.'

'Right, sir,' Dinesh clicked his heels and saluted Kamal.

Kamal turned and groaned as he saw the constables stepping out of the now working elevator.

Chapter 12

Aryan pulled the cap low over his face and threw caution to the winds. He should not have been here. Every neuron in his body screeched at him that it was a terrible idea.

He had been scouring the internet for the last twenty-four hours without a break for news about Roy. He knew it was only a matter of time before they found the body, but it had happened sooner than he had anticipated. The news of his death had been broken by the afternoon of the next day—barely sixteen hours. Turns out Roy's real name was Rohan Yadav. Aryan had the fleeting realisation of how little he knew about Roy.

But he knew enough. He had raped and killed Rashmi. Everything else about him was irrelevant. If he had any siblings, if his parents were still around to mourn him, what would happen to the stuff that he had left behind in his dingy drug den of an apartment. All Aryan knew was that Roy was in no way better than him. Roy's death was an accident, the more Aryan thought about it. But Roy's crimes were not. He knew exactly what he was doing, and he did it anyway. Hell, he gloated about it.

Aryan saw the full video over and over again once he woke up. There was no doubt, no guilt, no remorse in his face. There was no way it was the first time. Aryan shuddered to think how many times Roy had done this before. Whether there was a long list of other videos on his phone, just like Rashmi's. Kept as trophies, as souvenirs.

He deserved to die, Aryan reasoned with himself. He was not thrilled it happened by his hands, but he wasn't guilty either anymore. And then there were others…

He walked quickly, with his hands deep in his pockets and his chin stuck to his chest. Unlike his expectations, Hauz Khas Village was not a ghost town during the day. Just like any other colony, there were people walking about, going to shops, to work, and visiting neighbours. If anyone saw him around Roy's car, things would get very difficult for him very quickly.

He shook his head and took deep breaths to calm himself down. He needed Roy's phone. It was still in his car, where Deepak had left it that night, exactly as they had planned. However, with the video and Roy's death, everything had changed now. It would have contacts of Shiv, maybe more clues about who the third guy was. The police were going to be there any minute now, especially if Roy's phone was still on. He needed to get in and get out before anyone came.

He walked to the back of the car, where Deepak had dropped the keys, kicking them a foot or so under the car. Stroke of luck Deepak had not locked the keys inside the car. Aryan would have been locked out if he had. Still a risky move, Aryan thought to himself, exposing himself so close to the crime scene. He pulled out his handkerchief and carefully wrapped it around his hand. Gloves would be too suspicious, especially during the day when people could see him.

He fished around for the key and found it under the axle. It was a remote key, one which made a loud beep when you unlocked the car with it. Aryan felt beads of sweat crowding his brow. This was not going according to the plan at all. He looked around to see if someone was looking his way. Even if they were, he had no choice. He couldn't leave the phone there. The police would find it and put it in evidence, and he would lose the one lead he had to get to Shiv and whoever that other bastard was.

Throwing one last look around and gritting his teeth, he unlocked the car, holding his breath as if doing that would have made the beep quieter. The car's headlights flashed and there was a soft click that told him that the doors had unlocked. He quickly opened the passenger's side door and grabbed the phone and shoved it deep in his pocket. It had died already, so that was a relief. He left the key plugged into the ignition and locked the door manually. He peered in through the windows and made sure that the key was visible and once he was sure he had covered everything, he turned to leave as quickly as he could.

He turned and suddenly his stomach dropped to his feet. Right in front of him, about fifty feet away at the bend in the road, police officers were making the turn towards Roy's car, right where Aryan was standing. His eyes met the officer and for a second, Aryan saw a prison cell pass by in front of his eyes. He broke away the eye contact and walked in the opposite direction, his head down and cap pulled low.

'Hey you!' A loud, authoritative voice rang out behind him. Aryan walked on as if he had not heard anything.

'Oye! Red cap! Come here,' the voice grew louder. It was closer this time.

Aryan stopped and turned as slowly as he could. He saw a slightly potbellied, slightly balding police officer in his thirties walking briskly towards him.

'What were you doing near the car?'

'What?'

'The car. I saw you. You were looking inside.'

'Nothing.'

'Liar! You are a car thief, aren't you? Whose gang are you with? Munna? I know your entire clan,' the man grew louder and got within an arm's reach.

'What? No! That is my friend's car. I was looking for him,' Aryan spluttered out, not liking a word coming out of his mouth.

'Which friend?'

'Roy,' Aryan managed to choke out.

'How do you know Roy?' Kamal's eyes narrowed in suspicion.

'I met him at the club a couple of times. He asked me to meet him today. But he is late,' Aryan spoke, hoping the quivering in his voice was lost to the policeman.

'What is your name?'

Aryan quickly ran through the scenarios in his head. He could lie, but in that case if the cop asked for ID, he would catapult himself to a prime suspect in a second. If he told the truth however, he could be questioned later about the case. He gulped and replied.

'Aryan. Aryan Sinha.'

'Why did Roy want to meet you?'

'He...he had some scheme he wanted to tell me about. Some business he had invested in.'

Kamal scoffed. These good-for-nothing kids these days. Every other idiot was trying to make a quick buck with these multi-level marketing schemes.

'Well, Roy is dead. He had an accident yesterday. When was the last time you met him?'

'What? What do you mean he is dead?' Aryan tried to act shocked to the best of his modest acting abilities.

'He was found this morning, buried under a pile of bricks. When did you meet him last?'

'I am not sure. A week or so maybe. I ran into him in the village. He was leaving his shift at 'Anywhere' and I was leaving for home. We talked for a few minutes. I was a bit drunk, so he asked me to meet him today about this business opportunity.'

'What do you do?'

'I'm an artist. I work for a marketing firm as an animator.'

'Ok. Well, give this person your number and address,' Kamal pointed towards the constable, 'We will get in touch with you if we need any more information.'

'Of course,' Aryan nodded solemnly.

He dictated his number to the constable and started walking away quickly. He had to get out before there were any more questions. He was now in the circle. This was literally the worst thing that could have happened.

Unbeknownst to him, Kamal stared at him intently as he walked away. Aryan had severely underestimated what had just happened.

Chapter 13

Shiv Tandon stared at his phone. He could feel his heart race ahead, his shirt immediately sticking to his body in a cold sweat. He quickly threw a look around, no one was looking at him. He shot out of his chair and cubicle. Throwing looks over his shoulder, he walked to the bathroom, burying his phone deep in his pocket, as if it would explode if it came in contact with the cold air of his office. He entered a stall, locked the door behind him and sat down on the commode.

He took a few deep breaths to steady himself, pulled out his phone from his pocket and unlocked the screen—his clean-shaven face beamed back at him. The camera then panned downwards to reveal the girl he was on top of—some name starting with R. Rashmi, he thought to himself, not sure of the name. They had picked her up in Manali a year ago. The phone dropped from his hands as memories of that night came flooding back to him.

He sat there for a few minutes, with his head in his hands. He thought the video had been deleted. There was nothing tying him back to the whole thing. It was just the boys being stupid, they got carried away. He didn't need this to come back and haunt him now. He had just managed to put the whole thing behind him after almost a year of therapy.

His phone pinged again. He reached for it with shaking hands and looked at the screen. It was a text message from the same number which had sent him the video.

'I know what you did last summer,' the message taunted.

Shiv called back the number immediately. The call rang out and went unanswered. He called again. No answer again.

Shiv felt the bile rising in his throat and retched. Nothing came out. He suddenly felt very cold, like someone had sat him down inside a deep freezer on full blast. His hands shook so badly he could barely hold the phone steady. He looked at the video again, the thumbnail showing him smiling broadly at the camera, his naked body out of focus in the rest of the frame. He wiped his eyes and typed out a text.

'What is the meaning of this? Who are you?'

The screen changed to 'typing…'. Shiv waited with bated breath.

'Did you know rapists are the most hated kind of inmates in prisons? You are going to be in for ten years. You will last maybe six months.' the text popped back up.

Shiv called back again, furious, scared, anxious. The call went unanswered again. He tried calling from his phone instead of the app. Nothing again.

'I have no idea what you are talking about. I am blocking this number.' Shiv texted back. The screen immediately turned to 'typing… .'

'I dare you.'

The sender went offline. Shiv sank to the floor. He suddenly felt like he could not breathe. He pulled at his collar, gasping for air. Just then, a knock on the door startled him.

'Is everything fine? Do you need some help?'

Shiv peered from under the boot. He could see a pair of black sneakers out there. He cleared his throat to speak.

'Yeah. Yeah. Yes, I am ok. Thanks. Just slipped. I'll be right out.' Shiv called out.

The sneakers tottered for a while and then turned and walked out. Shiv waited till he heard the door close and then pulled himself to his feet. He deleted the video from his phone and gingerly opened the door. He walked out and splashed water on his face.

He looked into the mirror and could not even recognise himself. His face was pale under the perfectly trimmed beard, not an ounce of blood in his veins. His clothes, usually perfect, were now a mess, with wet patches from sitting on the floor of the stall. His eyes, a shiny shade of black, stared emptily into the reflection, not noticing anything around himself. He splashed more water on his face, trying to calm himself down. It was ok, he repeated to himself, he will get out of this.

He cursed the day he had met Roy.

Roy—it was all his fault, all his idea. He didn't even want to go to the club that night. It was all Roy. Shiv picked up his phone and called Roy. The phone was switched off. He looked at the time, two in the afternoon. He would be asleep right now. He would go see Roy at the club in the evening. They were all in this together. If he went down, he was not going alone. Roy would come with him. Shiv wondered if he could turn into the state's witness and save himself. He walked out of the bathroom, picked up his bag and left the office building. Getting into an auto idling in front of the office, not caring to negotiate the fare as always, Shiv texted out a half-assed excuse to his boss. He needed to get out of there, go back home, straighten his thoughts.

Aryan parked his car directly overlooking the gate of Shiv's office. It had taken him barely ten minutes to figure out Shiv's entire life history. Everything was logged in on Roy's phone. He had broken the original sim and was using VPN to access everything, while on a public network in one of the free Wi-Fi spots across the city. He was sure he was safe. Nothing would ever lead back to him.

Shiv Tandon—a mediocre engineer, an even worse software engineer, parents lived in Aligarh, one younger brother still in final year of high school. Shiv was a drifter, never staying at a job more than a few months. Aryan was amazed at what a fake profile on Facebook with a pretty girl's picture could let you find out about someone. Shiv had handed him everything on a plate—where he worked, who he knew, where he was most nights. Aryan watched an auto leave the campus and caught a glimpse of Shiv. He turned the key and slowly pulled into the traffic, a few hundred metres behind.

Ever since he had met the police at Roy's place, he always had a nagging voice in the back of his head asking him what he was doing. It was all a terrible idea. He had all the evidence. He could easily turn them in—send the video to the police, ask Deepak to file charges. He would not have to be anywhere in the picture. But he didn't want to.

He was constantly suppressing the voice in his head. He felt something driving him. Maybe it was Rashmi's last moments, all the pain she had to go through. Maybe it was his anger at these monsters taking her away from him, even though he had never really met her. Maybe it was the fear. No matter how he looked at it, he could not get himself to believe in ghosts. He was just hallucinating. Seeing things that were not there.

Rashmi had not dropped the bricks on Roy, it was an accident. Her spirit was not egging him to take revenge on her. It was stupid. But then, no matter how hard he tried, he could not wipe his memories clean. He knew what he had seen, and he had never been one to imagine things that were not there. He had, most definitely, seen Rashmi the night Roy died. But she was dead!

He could not come up with any explanation other than Rashmi's spirit coming back for revenge. He had been over this a thousand times without getting any closer to an answer. Maybe he was wrong and there was something to the stories his grandparents told him about ghosts, spirits, witches and demons. Maybe he was losing his mind. He would have to care about that later.

Aryan shook his head to clear his thoughts and stared ahead from behind the steering wheel.

Shiv's auto was pulling into a three-storeyed house squished in the middle of a row of similar houses. It was located in the sprawl of Malviya Nagar, a closely packed locality of the city, well known for cheap houses and good connectivity to the economic hubs of South Delhi. Aryan stopped his car at the end of the street and walked out casually. He stopped at the shop facing Shiv's house and bought a cigarette, though he hated the taste. He noted the address and wrote it down into a small spiral notebook. He thought about the logistics, this would not work. The place was too crowded. Nosy neighbours, houses where you could hear everything going on in the house next to you, across the thin walls. He would have to confront Shiv somewhere else, somewhere quieter.

Aryan looked at his watch. It was just about two in the afternoon. He stood there contemplating for a second. He did not want to hang around the place for too long. Even though Shiv had not been in touch with Roy for a while now, Aryan did not want to risk being seen again in case the police did show up to question Shiv. In any case, it did not look like Shiv was going to go anywhere for a while, given the state he had walked into his house. Aryan really wanted to know if Shiv was going to call the third guy, but it was not possible. All he could do now was wait. He decided to go back home and get some sleep. He had not realised how tiring stakeouts were. The last time, Deepak had been around to take shifts so they could take turns sleeping.

Aryan turned to his car, eyed the cigarette greedily and lit it up, if only to keep himself awake for long enough to make it back home safely. He sucked on the end gingerly and immediately felt his head swim. A novice smoker, he only managed to get a few drags in before he felt like he was going to fall over and stubbed it out. Walking to his car, Aryan practically fell on the driver's seat, still giddy from the nicotine. He took a few deep breaths and felt his head getting clearer. Collecting himself, he turned the key in ignition and drove away slowly.

Shiv latched the gate behind him as softly as he could and walked towards the main road. Malviya Nagar was a maze of streets and alleys, and it was only one in four times that you found an auto waiting for you right in front of your house. Most of the time, you would have to walk to one of the wider roads, just wide enough to allow two cars to pass each other, to find a transport to commute to the rest of the city. With his barely five-figure salary, Shiv could not afford his own vehicle and so usually ended up taking public transport everywhere.

He hailed an auto for the Saket Metro Station but was too dazed to perform the ritual haggling with the driver over the ten extra rupees that inevitably all auto drivers tried to get out of their passengers. He sat there, rocking in the auto as it navigated the potholed roads of the inner colony, lost in his own thoughts.

He cursed the day he had met Roy. With his well-built body, glamourous job and devil-may-care attitude, Roy had quickly left Shiv star struck. He always knew what to say to a woman in a club, on the streets, in a mall, outside the metro station. He wore fancy watches, lived in the most happening part of the town—it was a dream life for Shiv from where he stood.

It was perhaps these rose-tinted glasses that had blinded Shiv to what a psychopath Roy truly was. In the few months that he had spent hanging around Roy, he could not recall Roy ever referring to a woman as anything other than "bitch". He was like a predator, hunting drunk, solitary women in the streets of Hauz Khas Village where consent was only a passing concern. Shiv had always known that he needed to walk away, but couldn't. He was mesmerised by the life he knew he could never lead. Where he was sleeping with attractive women every night of the week, working barely a few hours a day and still making enough money to do whatever he damn well pleased. Like all psychopaths, Roy knew exactly what made Shiv tick and gave him just enough of a taste to keep on the leash, salivating for more.

Before he knew it, Shiv was right at the deep end. Roy had gone over unethical to strictly illegal territories, and Shiv had stood there, with a million excuses in his head along with bullshit ideas about gender, women, and drugs. And then, one day, over a year ago, in Manali, it all came crashing down on him.

Shiv closed his eyes and counted down from fifty, a technique taught by his therapist for evading panic attacks. He still went into a tizzy anytime he thought about Manali. He got out of the auto, slapped his wallet at the turnstile to enter the metro and took the yellow line to the Hauz Khas Station.

He reached the village and made his way to 'Anywhere', the club Roy worked at. It was still early, before the dinner rush, so maybe he would get a couple of minutes to talk to Roy. Maybe they could then go to his place and talk it over, see what they could do about it. Maybe Roy would have an idea how the video got leaked. Shiv felt anger rising in him. Roy had promised him that he had deleted the video. They should not have made the video in the first place. Fucker couldn't live without showing off.

He walked briskly to the club, his eyes unwavering. He was here for a job. Once this whole mess was sorted out, he would have enough time to look around and take in the scenery. Shiv had given it a lot of thought. He had a hunch that Roy was loaded. On his own part, he had maybe a few thousands in savings. If it came to blackmail, he would be helpless. He just didn't have the money. He could not turn to anyone for help, considering what he had done and the mess he was in. The only way out he could see was roping Roy in with him. It was his idea in the first place. It was only fitting that he faced the consequences too. Why should Shiv be the only one suffering?

He got lost a couple of times, he had not been there in months, but eventually managed to find the place. However, as he approached the place, he felt something was off. Even though it was early, the club looked bare. There were hardly any people around, which was never the case anywhere in the village once the sun began to set. But here it was, looking bare as a billiard ball.

Police! There were two bikes with red and blue number plates parked in front of the club. A few constables milled around, asking questions to *paan* shops around the area and talking to bouncers. Shiv immediately stopped dead in his tracks and turned around. Shit! Have the police already reached Roy? Was the footage out? What he had received was only a clip of it, barely half a minute long. But Roy was in it for most of the runtime.

Shiv started walking away slowly, looking at his feet. He had to get out as quickly as he could. Not looking where he was going, he bumped into a young guy with big, black facial hair, knocking him off his feet.

'Watch where you are going, will you?' the guy said angrily.

Shiv mumbled out a sorry and extended his hand. Still muttering, he took his hand and hoisted himself back up.

'It's bad enough the police are messing up the business, now I got to deal with this too? Who is going to pay my rent?'

Shiv's eyes lit up. This was his chance! He could find out what was going on.

'What has happened?'

'Some stupid bullshit. Some bartender in that club has gone missing. Hmph. Looks like a case of runaway. I knew the guy. Always fucking around. Must have fucked somebody important's daughter. Or wife. Who the fuck can tell these days.'

'Roy?'

'Yeah, I think that was his name. Something like that only. Never liked the bastard.'

'Why are the police looking for him?' Shiv pressed.

'How would I know? Someone must have filed a complaint or something. He realised he was in trouble so took off. Will be back in a couple of months probably. Or not. Who can even tell these days.'

Shiv felt his throat close around his heart. Roy was gone! 'Oh. Well, sorry. I hope you are not hurt.' Shiv offered politely before pushing past the man.

'Keep your eyes about you, you knock down a cop like this and next thing you know, your parents will be looking for you,' the man yelled after him, guffawing rudely.

Shiv pushed him out of his head and walked quickly with his head bent down. He had to get out too. Staying in Delhi was too dangerous for him. Who knew how long it would be before the police came looking for him, even in Aligarh. That was the first place they would look. He needed a plan, and he needed it quickly.

He could feel a migraine coming. It didn't look like it was going to be an easy night for him.

Aryan smiled to himself, scratching his chin under the itchy, cheap beard he had bought for a hundred bucks from an actor near Mandi House.

Shiv had bought it. Hook. Line. Sucker.

Chapter 14

'I told you it wasn't an accident!' Kamal exclaimed loudly.

Dinesh, who had just entered the room, looked up in surprise to see Kamal leaning back on his chair with a smug smile on his face, palms behind his head, the report from the forensic lab laid open in front of him on his desk.

'Take a look. There was Propofol in his blood. He had been drugged. It is not a recreational thing. It is used in surgeries to knock people out.' Kamal continued, staring at the ceiling.

Dinesh walked up to the table and looked at the report. Death from blunt force trauma to the head. The neck had been snapped, bent the wrong way from the weight of the bricks. There were several other fractures of varying severity across the body. Dinesh scanned through the list. At least three of them would have been fatal on their own.

'Ok. So, it was not an accident. But then, why make it so complicated?' Dinesh replied, putting the file back in front of Kamal.

'Look at the facts here. We find a young guy dead in

the middle of nowhere, in a building, nonetheless. Why a building? Why not a farm? Why not some forgotten canal out in Western UP? It would be much easier to hide a body there. If not that, at least it would take us a few days to find the body. Enough to muddle all the evidence. Then why in a building?' Kamal spoke, not looking at Dinesh, his eyes still stuck to the ceiling.

'It was desolate. No one was around. It was convenient.'

'Exactly,' Kamal shot up straight and walked to the white board on the wall opposite him, 'It was convenient. Why was it convenient? Maybe the place was familiar to the people who were there with Yadav.'

'He preferred Roy,' Dinesh said softly.

'Yeah, yeah, whatever. Roy. The point is that it gives us a clue. The person who was there that night with Roy had a connection to the building. He knew when it would be empty. He knew how to work the elevators. He knew the layout. That's a start.'

'Is it though? What if it was just convenient because it was empty?'

'You think this is not a premeditated crime? You don't get Propofol at the corner pharmacy. No, of course someone planned the whole thing. Knocked Roy out, took him to a familiar place, then killed him.'

'Then why not kill him directly?' Dinesh said, looking at the scribbles Kamal was making on the white board.

'I don't know. Maybe, they wanted some information from him. He was a bartender, and they meet all sorts of people. Maybe he was in too deep with the wrong sort of people. Maybe, the place was making a statement, a hint of flair before the murder. Do one thing.'

'What?' Dinesh jerked his head up.

'Check on Roy. See if he has a history with drugs or something sketchy. Not just our records, which are mostly clean anyway, but people around him. Check who were the people he used to hang around with and get a list of all the people who have had access to the building in the last one month. Everyone—workers, engineers, buyers, agents, contractors—leave no one out. We will start from there. The second there is a common name between the two lists, we are done.'

Dinesh nodded solemnly. It made sense. In any case, he had no interest in keeping the case open longer than he needed to. So, whatever kept Kamal off his back. He got up and started walking out.

'One more thing.' Kamal called out.

'Yes, sir?'

'Where is his phone?'

'Phone?'

'Yeah. It was not with him. It was not at his house. Where did his phone go?'

'Well, we got his number from one of the neighbours and tried calling, but it was switched off. Dead battery or something.'

'Get me his phone records. When was the last time he used it, when it was last switched on, all that. Get me everything from the last three months.'

'Alright, sir.' Dinesh clicked his heels in salute and walked out.

Kamal stared at the white board in front of him, gathering his thoughts. Roy was last seen at 10.30 pm at a mall with his friends. He left alone and was dead before five in the morning. During this time, he was drugged and kidnapped, maybe even tortured. Kamal suppressed a guilty gleeful smile as he delved deeper and deeper into it. What had started out as a construction accident was turning a lot more interesting very quickly.

Chapter 15

Aryan lit his fifth cigarette of the day. It was quickly turning into an addiction, and he was not liking it. But he liked the clarity it gave him. He needed his wits about him. He was deep in a dangerous game, and he needed to think through every possibility. Shiv had been calling the burner phone incessantly. Aryan had to plan everything to the T to pull this off.

Aryan took a deep drag and let the smoke burn its way down his lungs. He held his breath and let the nicotine wash over his senses. He could feel his heartbeat rise ever so slightly and the voice in his head quiet down. It still made his head swim.

Shiv had done exactly what he had expected him to do. He had not gone to the police. Obviously. Rape was much worse than getting blackmailed. Aryan did not have to worry about Shiv bringing in outside help. There was no version of this where Shiv came off as the victim. He was trapped and he knew it. There was a possibility that he had reached out to the third guy, but Aryan had no way of knowing that. He had been keeping an eye on Shiv's apartment, but he barely left it, and had certainly had no visitors. If he had called the third person, well, there was not much Aryan could have done about it. Maybe it would be a good thing. He just might get both together.

Aryan was startled by his doorbell. He quickly glanced at the clock. It was around seven thirty in the evening. He was not expecting anyone. He stubbed the cigarette out on the floor and stalked to the door. Aryan opened it to find a fuming Akshay standing there, his laptop slung over one shoulder. He stepped back and let Akshay in.

'Where the hell have you been?' Akshay fumed the second door was closed.

Aryan turned to face him. He did not have time for this. He had to text Shiv in about fifteen minutes. He needed to get rid of Akshay quickly.

'You have missed work for three days straight. You don't pick up your cell. No one knows why you are not coming. Wait, is that a cigarette?'

Aryan quickly brushed the butts under the dresser with his foot and walked into the kitchen, mostly to avoid facing Akshay.

'Dude don't walk away. What the fuck is going on? Are you on drugs or something?'

'What? No. Why would you think that?' Aryan shot back.

'Well, I don't know what the fuck to think anymore, do I? You suddenly just vanish from work one day, no information, not even to me. When the boss asks me where you are, what am I supposed to tell him? Do you have any idea how difficult it was to cover for you?'

'I am sorry. Things have just been crazy the last few days.'

'Yeah? And why is that?'

I watched the ghost of a girl kill the man who raped her, Aryan thought to himself, getting more and more comfortable with forming the idea in his head. It did not seem all that crazy anymore. He had spent the hours between tormenting Shiv and researching on paranormal cases. The internet was full of stories much crazier than this. He might have dismissed them as stories or delusions once upon a time, but now with all that had happened to him, he couldn't help but see those once ridiculous stories in a new light.

'It's...it is complicated.' Aryan stammered.

'Yeah? Try me,' Akshay shot back angrily.

Aryan stood there tottering on his toes, stealing glances at the wall clock. Ten minutes.

'I don't know dude, there is just something going on. I can't explain it. It is just very complicated.'

'Is it about that Rashmi thing?' Akshay's eyes narrowed.

Aryan gulped instead of answering.

'Are you fucking kidding me?' Akshay exploded.

'Dude. She is dead. You did not meet her. It's not possible. It was a crazy coincidence. People resemble others all the time. Get a grip on yourself. What the fuck is wrong with you?'

Aryan felt a fury rising in him slowly. He took a deep breath to calm himself down.

'You are right. It's not that. There is some stuff going with my family. I'm sorry I got you worried.'

'What stuff? Tell me. I can help.'

'It's fine man. Really. I will figure it out. I'll be back tomorrow. Promise.'

'Yeah? Ok. Come with me then.'

'What?'

'Yes. I don't trust you. You are smoking now. And I am pretty sure you just lied to me. So, that's it. You are coming with me. We'll go to work together tomorrow. Pack your clothes.'

'Dude, stop it. It's not necessary.' Aryan said, his voice a low growl now.

'Well, I don't give a shit. You are coming with me.'

'FUCK YOU!' It was Aryan's turn to shout. Akshay looked stunned.

'There is no need to try and be my father,' Aryan continued, 'I told you I will be there. That's it. I have said all I had to. Leave now.'

Akshay stood there, blinking in shock for a second. Then without a word, he slung his bag over his shoulder and walked out. Aryan held the door open for him.

Akshay turned once he was out of the door. Aryan felt a pang of guilt on seeing Akshay's face. He looked genuinely hurt.

'I am just worried about you man. This is not like you. You have changed.' Akshay said softly, looking into Aryan's eyes.

'More has changed than you will ever realise,' Aryan said slowly and shut the door right on Akshay's face.

Two minutes to go. He had a text to send.

Chapter 16

Shiv stared at the text on his phone, the knot in his chest finally easing just a little after days of agony.

'Hi. It's me. No names or details on text. I had to leave the city. You know why. We need to talk.'

Roy! Finally! It was an unknown number. Clearly new, possibly a friend's. So, Shiv's hunch was right. The blackmailer had got to Roy too and he skipped town. It made sense.

'What about our other friend? Does he know?' Shiv looked at the text he had typed. It was vague enough, he decided, and pressed send.

'Yes. Don't contact him on the phone. He will be joining us. Come to Sonipat tomorrow and call on this number. We must talk in person.'

Sonipat. Shiv knew vaguely that Roy was from Haryana, but he never found out where exactly. It just never came up. He must be at his home right now, tapping into his local network and resources to solve this problem. Maybe, he knew people in police, even local politicians. That would certainly help.

The icon on top of the screen changed again as Roy started to type. A second later a message popped up again.

'Come to the bus stand at eleven tomorrow morning. A guy will pick you up and bring you here. We need to figure this out quickly. Delete these messages.'

Shiv stared hard at the phone. Roy was acting strange, a bit too paranoid maybe. Why did he ask him to delete the messages? It did not feel right to him. He took screenshots of the conversation and uploaded them to his cloud drive. Just a second later the messages vanished. Roy had deleted them from his end. Shiv was glad that he had taken the screenshots. This was all the evidence he had to protect himself anyway in case Roy turned on him. It was not much but it was better than nothing.

He looked at the clock. It was just about eight in the night. Sonipat was not far. It would take him less than two hours to reach. He would leave early in the morning, take a bus from ISBT. Or maybe a train. That would be safer. He suddenly regretted not having a car. He vaguely wondered if it would have been cheaper to get one instead of taking a cab everywhere.

Shiv spent a sleepless night, turning in his bed, going over every bad decision he had made which had led him to this point. Meeting Roy, getting seduced by his life, letting him call the shots, following his lead even when every ounce of his fibre screamed at him to run in the opposite direction. Where had all that led him? To this place, where he was getting blackmailed, and if he didn't play it right, he would end up in a prison.

A prison. His father would have a heart attack for sure. The man didn't have as much as a parking ticket in his life. He wasn't sure if his mother even knew the concept of jails, courts and sentences. She had led a quiet, unintrusive life, living in the shadow of the men in her extended family—every decision made for her by someone else. There was no one he could turn to for help. Doing so would mean accepting, even if in parts, to the horrible things he let happen, things he had done.

Shiv rolled out of bed just at daybreak, unable to sleep anymore and got dressed. He charged his phone and slipped a portable power bank in his bag, just in case. He checked his wallet, just a little over a thousand rupees. He would stop at an ATM on his way. He had a separate account he had just started maintaining, with maybe around twenty thousand rupees. Enough for a trip to Sonipat, but not much else. If it came to paying off the blackmailer, the amount would be ridiculous. He locked the door behind him, fighting an ominous feeling for some inexplicable reason.

Aryan sat at a small tea shop right outside the bus stand and waited. He had parked his car a few hundred metres down the road, close enough to make a quick getaway, once it was all done, but too far to be tied to him. He checked his phone, another fake number, his own phone was back in Delhi, strengthening his alibi of being at home. He had set it up to order food to his apartment twice during the day. It was not enough but could be defended in case things went south.

He watched the place through his dark glasses. It was not much of a disguise, but it would do. It was a bus stand.

Thousands of people went through it every day. No one would remember him. He wore a nondescript white kurta and black jeans. He had bought them on his way here from a small shop along the highway, one which did not believe in bills or paying taxes. He had a change of clothes in his car, another in his bag. Aryan had been reading incessantly all sorts of message boards on the internet, which gave advice of the sort. It was amazing what you could find in the dark alleyways of the world wide web. He obsessively memorised tricks of the trade, practicing more and more as he learnt them, like a novice pianist, butchering piece after piece, convinced of her virtuosity.

It was just about eleven. The harsh Haryana sun beat down on him, somehow feeling hotter than the one he saw in Delhi. The bus stand was dusty, crowded and loud. It would have made anyone but an Indian choke and have a panic attack. There was a thin mist of dust, raised by buses plying on the semi-paved roads leading to the bus stand. Any moment now, he glanced at time. Buses from Delhi came at an indecent frequency, reminding people in this sleepy town that there was a great big world out there, of the inadequacy of their own town. He did not expect Shiv to be punctual. It was impossible to tell when a bus would reach when you got on one. It could be annoyingly early, or fashionably late.

It was around twenty past eleven when an incoming bus caught his attention. It had a Delhi number plate and was not teeming with people like the others. Probably it still believed in the fiction of tickets and reservations, something that was a luxury in a poor, overpopulated country like India. He rose and walked to a corner from where he could get a clear view of the passengers. People filed out from the bus, young men with sunglasses, old women with an umbrella jutting from their jute handbags. Shiv was the last person to get down. Aryan recognised him instantly. He had not taken any efforts to disguise himself. Not even a pair of sunglasses. Fool, Aryan thought to himself.

Aryan saw Shiv taking a look around for a second before fishing his phone out of his pocket. Sure enough, a few seconds later, Aryan's phone chimed. He walked out of the corner, checked his reflection in a bus window, pulled his cap low over his face and turned towards Shiv.

The phone rang for a full ring and a half and then disconnected. Shiv squinted at it. Great! Roy had asked him to call him once he reached Sonipat and now won't pick up his call. He mashed the call button again just when he heard a voice from over his shoulder.

'Shiv Tandon?'

'Yes.'

'Roy sent me to pick you up. Switch off your phone and hand it here, first thing they will look at', he said, waiting for a second and looking around before continuing, 'Where is the other guy?'

'Which other guy?' Shiv looked up, asking over the chime of his phone turning off.

'I was supposed to pick two of you up. Where is the other one?'

'I don't know. I came alone,' Shiv stiffened, as he handed over his phone. He knew who the third guy was. So, Roy had called all of them after all.

'Son of a... Fine. We will wait.'

'He is not here already. I am a bit late.' Shiv asked, slinging his bag over his shoulder.

'You tell me. He was supposed to come with you.'

'No, he wasn't,' Shiv protested, 'Roy asked me... .'

'No names, you idiot. Wait till we get out of here,' the man snarled.

'You took my name,' Shiv replied testily.

'Well, is your father the sarpanch? Yeah. I thought not. Come on. I will come back for him later.'

'Are you sure? He must be on his way.'

'Yeah. why don't you wear a board around your neck you fuckwit? It's bad enough as it is what you bastards have done. You want to hang around the busiest place in town and announce it to everyone too now?'

Shiv looked at his feet. So, he knew. The rising shame in Shiv suddenly made him a lot more compliant.

'Come on.'

The guy stuck out his arm and hailed an auto. It was already half full. Shiv sat on the rear seat while the guy sat beside the driver, perched precariously on the edge of the seat. A verifiably small-town skill.

They rode in silence for about fifteen minutes, the auto was too loud to have a conversation anyway. They went through the wide main road and got off near the edge of the city.

'Come on. We are here,' the guy announced and hopped off, stretching. Shiv got off gingerly.

They were on the road leading out of the city, surrounded by farms on all sides. The road sloped off on either side a couple of feet into the farmlands, making sure it would not drown when the heavy July rains arrived. They got off the road on a dirt path and walked deeper into the fields.

'Where are we going?,' Shiv asked, slightly uneasy. He had just now realised that he was following a complete stranger into the middle of the fields out in the wilderness of Haryana.

'We can't go to the house. It is too risky. This would be safer,' the guy replied pointing towards a *khalihan*. It was large, maybe enough to house a tractor or even a combiner if you knew how to park it.

Shiv followed the guy into the shed. It was made from straws strung over a scaffolding of bamboo. The ceiling was rather high, maybe fifteen feet and despite the harsh sun outside, it was somewhat pleasant inside. The air was stuffy but cool and the dirt floor had been sprinkled with water giving the place a gentle petrichor. There were a few woven stools in a corner, a wooden chair and a charpoy in one corner. In the other corner, there was an earthen pot and a ladle-like glass with a long handle on top of the lid. It took Shiv a few seconds to realise it, as his eyes adjusted to the dim light, that the place was empty.

'Where is Roy?' He spun around to face the other guy.

'He will come once the two of you are here. Safer that

way. If anyone sees him coming in, they will stop to give their regards or whatever. I wanted to do it at night, but he was being an ass about it.'

Shiv walked to one of the stools and sat down.

'Wait here. I will go pick up the other one. Don't leave. And make sure no one sees you. Roy's family owns this land. There will be questions.'

Shiv nodded softly. The other guy walked out and dragged the bamboo door close behind him, making a scraping sound on the door floor below, leaving Shiv in the darkness.

Aryan left the shed, walked a few hundred metres till he was out of sight and sat on his haunches under a tree. It had taken him a good while to find this place. He had spent the last two days asking around the city, apparently this place was considered haunted, and the locals stayed clear of the place. It usually meant that desperate couples would come to fool around, if at all. During the day, and especially during the night, the place was bare for half a kilometre in all directions.

Once upon a time, the thought of staying in a haunted shed would have terrified him. Now, it didn't matter. He knew ghosts were real. Rashmi was real. He had seen her every night since in his dreams—in his nightmares. In his daydreams.

Every time all she demanded was revenge, as Aryan stood, stuck helplessly, sometimes in ice, sometimes under a landslide at the bottom of the ravine where he had first met her.

He lit a cigarette and took a drag. It was the cheap, local stuff he had bought on the bus stand. The rough tobacco made his throat burn. He persisted, more out of habit than anything. He was up to almost a pack every day by now. He finished it and carefully put the butt back in his pocket. He would throw it away maybe in his house, or somewhere down the road. It was an unnecessary precaution, avoiding leaving his DNA at the scene, but one that did not require much effort.

He sat there, thinking. He had something resembling a plan. The first part was easy. He had to find out who the third guy was. He knew the face, the images from the video seared into his mind. But he did not have a name. He had scoured Roy's friend list and phone, but there was no inkling of him. Unlikely that he was not on social media, but with Roy's profile as chock full as it was of fake profiles—Hero Rocky, Rajput Sher and Mr Seven Inches Deep—it was like looking for a needle in a haystack.

The thing that was still open was what he was going to do with Shiv. He was not going to kill him. Roy's death was an accident. He had considered turning him over to the police but with Roy's death, it would all tie back to him very easily right now. There was even a possibility that the third guy was very well connected and could manage to escape, pin it all on Shiv. It was a possibility, given how brazen their actions had been. In which case, all of this would be in vain, and the monster would still be out in the streets.

He could think about going to the police only if he had hard evidence. A confession that would be admissible in court was the only thing that would make the case watertight. Maybe it would also take the heat off him. If he could promise a conviction, maybe Rashmi's family would understand. Their daughter's killers would have finally been brought to justice.

He looked at the watch. It had been a little over twenty minutes and he had to return in another twenty. It was a reasonable time to make the trip and back. He carefully went over the script in his mind that he had been crafting for the last several days. He had to be crafty. If he could not coax the answer out, he would have to resort to harsher methods and he was not very enthused at the idea.

Unbeknownst to him, the solution to the final part of his problem was lurking close by.

Chapter 17

'Something is not adding up,' Kamal spoke loudly, startling Dinesh who was sitting opposite to him.

'What do you mean, sir?'

'The timelines. They don't add up.'

'Sir?'

'Yeah. Think about it. Roy meets his friends for a movie. Movie ends at 8.30. They eat and Roy leaves for his house at around ten. He reaches home and stays there till three in the night as per his phone records, then the phone switches off. But the forensic report puts his time of death between four and six in the morning. To get to the murder scene from his house would take about forty minutes easily, maybe even half an hour if it's night and the roads are clear. So, somehow, between three and six, he manages to get drugged and killed, twenty kilometres from his place. How is that possible?'

Dinesh stared at the file in front of him. He had to complete the report before evening. He did not have time for this hair splitting.

'I don't know, sir.' He replied curtly and returned his attention to the report.

'We didn't find his phone at his house, right?'

'No, sir. We looked everywhere. It is still switched off, maybe even the sim card has been removed because it alternates between switched off and out of network coverage area.'

'Hmm. We have the footage of his car leaving the mall, right?'

'Yes, sir. Clearly. The resolution is not great, but the make and colour of his car is clear. He left right on time.'

'No CCTV footage from the car park, right?'

'No, sir. All the cameras were out of order for weeks. The assholes never fixed it.'

'Remind me to fuck them over with this. Anyway, so he received some calls but never picked up any. He went home and suddenly ended up dead. That does not make sense.'

'What if we have it wrong?'

'What do you mean?'

'I mean sir, what if he never went home? There are no witnesses to him returning home. His landlord said that he always keeps an eye out and he said that he did not hear him come back.'

'And someone else drove his car back, while he was kidnapped.'

'I guess so.'

'Remember that kid? The one we caught hanging around his house.'

'Yeah. Some Sinha.'

'Call him once. What if he was not there to meet Roy, but to check if we knew.'

'Isn't that a bit of a stretch, sir?'

'Is it? We found the key to Roy's car inside the car. If Roy came back, why would he lock his keys inside? It is a very difficult thing to do by mistake. The records aren't that accurate. What if the phone was in the car, and not Roy. He never came back. Someone drove his car home and left it there.'

Dinesh considered the possibility. It did not make complete sense to him yet, but it sure felt a little sketchy. He decided it was best to go along with it.

'Ok, sir. I will call him.'

'Yeah, ask him to come to the station tomorrow morning. Let's see if this kid knows anything. If nothing else, we can take a statement from him. And check with Roy's friends. See if any of them drove the car back or something. I need a clear chain of events from all the witnesses for the night.'

'Sure, sir. I will get to it,' Dinesh sighed, looking longingly at his report.

Roy was making more people sad in his death than he had in his life.

Chapter 18

The other guy burst through the door. Shiv was sitting in the same spot where he had left him, staring blankly at the wall in front of him.

'He is still not here,' he said loudly.

'What?' Shiv looked up, broken out of his reverie.

'The other guy, who was supposed to be there, whats-his-name.'

'Oh.'

He waited for a couple of seconds. Shiv fell back into silence.

'Well, that is all you have to say-*Oh?* That is rich! First you idiots get yourself in this mess and I am here, leaving everything, trying to fix it and all I get is an *Oh?*' he yelled.

Shiv looked up, slightly nervous now. He balled up his fingers, hoping that the twitch in his fingers was not visible.

'Do you have his number?'

'Whose?'

'The third guy with you. Roy is not coming till both of you are here and I don't have all day. I have got things to do, alright?'

'I don't know what you are talking about,' Shiv said slowly, looking away, the quiver in his voice noticeable.

'Cut the shit wiseass. I know what the three of you did. I saw the video. Don't bullshit me,' Aryan continued, his voice louder, more frustrated now.

'Don't you have his number? You had mine,' Shiv asked, challenging Aryan, looking at him for the first time since he had walked in.

'I don't. He told me both of you are coming at eleven and to pick up both of you,' the other guy fumed.

Shiv didn't reply. For the first time since he had arrived, he felt panic. Something was not adding up.

'What do we do now?' Shiv asked.

'There's no we here. I am done and I will be leaving in half an hour, irrelevant of who is here. Roy can figure out his mess all by himself. I am done cleaning up after this fucker,' he said and pulled out his phone.

'Well, I suppose I can give you his number,' Shiv replied after a few seconds, unsure of himself.

'Then why didn't you do that to begin with? If he is not coming, I will tell Roy and he can figure out what he wants to do. I don't have time to stand around all day. I am not his henchman.'

'I wasn't sure', Shiv replied.

'Well, I don't care. Give me the number.'

'It's there on my phone. Look it up.'

'Don't you remember it? I don't want to switch on your phone here,' he shot back.

'Fine,' Shiv dictated the number out loud from memory, 'His name is Abhishek. Abhishek Dhingra. Tell him Shiv is waiting for him in Sonipat and ask him whether he is coming.'

'Ok. Wait here. Let me go speak to him,' the other guy replied and left the room.

Shiv felt the knot in his throat ease a little. He cursed himself softly for giving up his phone in the morning to the other guy. At least he should have tried to find out his name. If Shiv had kept the phone with himself, he would not have been in this mess.

A few minutes passed before the other guy walked into the room, looking confused. Shiv knew it had worked.

'Whose number did you give me?'

'Abhishek Dhingra. He now knows where I am,' Shiv offered, more casually than he felt.

'What the fuck are you talking about?' The other guy was taken aback.

'Yes. Now there are people who know where I am. You can't pull anything anymore. I know you are lying. Where is Roy? And who are you?'

The other guy stood there stunned, unable to speak for a minute. Shiv felt a wave of relief wash over him. Abhishek had the number. He knew where he was. If anything went wrong, they could track him down. It was his insurance and it seemed to be working.

'You dense motherfucker!' the other guy spoke after a minute through gritted teeth. 'You have any idea what you have done?'

'Foiled your plans, it seems to me.'

'No Einstein. You have declared to people that you are here, in Roy's hometown. If the blackmailing scum, whoever it is, finds out about it he knows that you are meeting Roy. How long do you think it will take him to release the video and then vanish?'

'What are you talking about?'

'You idiot. Why do you think Roy left town? And why did he call you here? He called you here because he knew that the blackmailer was following him and staking out his house to make sure he didn't go to the police. When he left, he probably started keeping an eye on your house because Roy went off the grid. This is why we called you out here to talk, so that you all can plan how to deal with it without the blackmailer finding out about it. Now you have announced to people that you are in Sonipat. If your darling roommate decides to come here to find you, how long do you think it will take the blackmailer to figure that out?'

Shiv forgot how to breathe for a second. His head was bursting and he sank down to the stool. This went much deeper than he realised. It was not just someone casually messing around with him. It was a plan to bring them down. Out of the corner of his eye, he saw the other guy turn and walk towards the door.

'Where are you going?' Shiv yelled after him.

'I am leaving. I am not going down with you guys as an accomplice or whatever. Roy's father is a politician, mine is not. I am not getting involved. You fuckers are on your own,' he said, dragging the door open.

'No, wait. I am sorry. Please, get me to talk to Roy once,' Shiv pleaded.

'Here's your phone. Call him,' the other guy threw Shiv's phone at him, 'You have the number. Do what you want. I am done.'

'No. Wait. Please. I'll call him.'

Shiv switched on the phone and quickly scrolled to Roy's number and called. It was switched off. He called the number which he had received Roy's text from. It rang in the other guy's pocket.

'I have that number you idiot. Do you have any idea how difficult it is to get fake numbers anymore? I am not getting my name involved in your mess.'

'Wait. Please. Just one more minute. I'll call Vikram.'

'Right! Call him. See what good it does you. If he has any sense, he would have switched his phone off and ran halfway to Bhutan by now. You are the only one here who is getting fucked. I hope it was worth it.'

Shiv ignored the jab and scrolled down his contact list. The last time he had called this number was a year ago. More than that, in fact. He had broken off all contact after that night. After he had seen him do what he did.

'It's ringing,' Shiv announced. The other guy simply stood there, staring at him, his hands fidgeting in his pocket.

'Hello! Vikram! It's me, Shiv. You are not coming?' Shiv rattled off the second Vikram picked up the call.

The other guy moved closer, his hands still in his pocket.

'What do you mean where? Sonipat. Roy called you, right?'

Shiv spoke urgently, unsure if he had heard him correctly.

'Roy...is dead? What…' Shiv's eyes widened as he saw a glint of metal around the other guy's fingers before it crashed into the side of his head. His phone went flying out of his head and he crashed to the ground, barely feeling the stickiness on the side of his head.

The other guy calmly walked to the phone, picked it up, switched it off and pocketed it.

'Finally! I thought you were never going to make that call!' He smiled evilly at Shiv.

Shiv's eyes widened in shock as the other guy pulled back his fist to hit him again.

'Stop,' Shiv spluttered out, choking back saliva and blood, 'Abhishek knows I am here.'

'Please! I knew he was your roommate. First comment on your display picture. I never made the call,' the other guy grinned sinisterly.

His fist came crashing down on Shiv's face, right between his nose and lips. Everything immediately turned black.

Chapter 19

Manali
A Year Ago

Shiv scooped up the beers Roy had ordered and carried them to the table where he was sitting with another one of his friends, Vikram Bidhuri. He was thankful for Roy's tab on the bar, there was no way he could have afforded to get drunk in a nightclub like this. All the drinks, even the beers, cost at least half a day's salary.

He squeezed into the booth beside Roy, who clapped him hard on the shoulder and caused him to nearly spill the drinks.

'That's my boy. See Vikram, I told you? The boy has his uses,' Roy laughed raucously. Vikram looked at Shiv like he was vermin and picked up a mug. Shiv only smiled, unsure of how to respond.

'So, my boy. Tell me. See anything you like?' Roy took a large swig, already drunk.

'What do you mean?'

'For the night of course! How is that one in the red dress over there? She looks eager.'

'Aren't you here on a date?' Shiv asked in surprise.

'Well, if you can call it that,' Roy winked at Vicky, who smirked.

'What do you mean?' There was something non-verbal going on between Roy and Vikram that Shiv did not understand.

'Patience, young student. Patience. It is still too early. The club is not crowded enough. As with everything else, timing is the most important part here. You get that right, everything else falls in place. Till then, sit back, relax, enjoy the view,' Roy said mysteriously and returned to his almost brown lager.

They sat there for about an hour, talking about random things, shooting the breeze. Shiv tried very hard to follow their conversation, but it was unintelligible to him. They spoke almost exclusively in abbreviations and even though Shiv had the vague sense that they were talking about women from the pronouns, he had absolutely no idea what exactly they were saying.

It was just over 9 pm when Vikram nodded to Roy, who nodded back and both turned around. Shiv turned with them but wasn't sure what they were looking for.

'Ten o'clock. Silver dress, red hair. Looks like a kamikaze shot in her hand,' Vikram said after scanning the room for a bit.

'No. Too much work, we need someone with a larger drink. A beer bottle preferably, or at least something dark coloured.'

'What are we talking about?' Shiv asked nervously. He did not want to come across like an idiot, but he had no idea what was going on here.

'We are looking for our date, of course.'

'Our?' Shiv raised an eyebrow.

'Yes. You see, it is an art. There are criteria that must be followed. You can't have guys in the group, they complicate things. I promise at least one of them is picturing himself on top of her tonight. So, you stay away from mixed sets. Best is no groups, but that doesn't happen a lot, so you look for small, all female groups, preferably where all are drinking.'

'Wow! You really have this figured out, don't you?' Shiv said, impressed for some reason that he could not articulate.

'Well, stick around. I have a lot to teach you,' Roy grinned. Vikram laughed obscenely.

'I will go do a round. Get your game face on,' Vikram stood up suddenly and walked off, his shoulders thrown back. Roy nodded and cracked his knuckles, looking excited.

'How do you choose who to hit on? What if she has a boyfriend or something?' Shiv pressed on. Roy's eyes were still stuck to the dance floor like a wolf.

'What does that have to do with anything?' Roy's eyes never leaving the floor.

'What do you mean? How will you hit on someone who has a boyfriend?'

'I can hit on whoever I please. There is or isn't a boyfriend is none of my concern. If she doesn't have a problem, why would I create a fuss?'

'What if she says no?'

'You are a kid. You will learn. Looks like Vikram is done. Sit straight and don't interrupt.'

Vikram slid into the booth and bent his head low over the table. Roy leaned in and Shiv followed suit, not sure what they were discussing that was so confidential.

'Found her. Probably a two set but I don't see the other one around. Dark blue dress. She is just sitting at the bar with a cosmopolitan. Go take your seat, centre of the bar. I'll wait for your signal.'

Roy nodded and left, walking towards the other side of the bar. Shiv was not sure he followed but was caught up in the excitement. It felt like they were spies, or secret agents, on an international mission to steal a microchip or some other McGuffin. Shiv and Vikram sat patiently in the booth, sipping warm beers now.

About fifteen minutes later, Vikram's phone buzzed. He quickly picked it up and looked at it.

'Ok. Here is what I need you to do,' Vikram turned towards Shiv. Shiv's ears perked up like a dog's, 'Here's my card, settle the bill and get everything cleared here. Get out of here in exactly ten minutes from now. Start the car, bring it up front and park it as close to the gate as possible. We will leave one by one. I will come first, Roy will come after that. We have twenty minutes from now. Let's go.'

Vikram quickly rose and walked out of sight towards the other end of the club, where Roy was. Shiv sat there a little disoriented, and a little bit drunk. He drank a glass of water, got up, and went with a waiter to the front desk to close the tab. He saw from the corner of his eye that Roy was talking to a pretty girl who was sitting at the bar, while Vikram was standing on the other side of her. For the briefest moment, Shiv thought he saw Vikram's hand over the girl's glass, but it was hard to tell anything from the distance.

Shiv walked out and took the keys from his pocket. It was an expensive sedan, worth probably more than five years of his salary at the very least. They had rented it in Delhi and drove to Manali—Roy and Shiv. Vikram had joined them here. Shiv had not been expecting the invitation at all. He had only met Roy a few times, and then hung out at his house drinking and smoking up once or twice. But Roy told him that the guy he was supposed to go with backed out at the last minute and he needed another driver. Already smitten with the lifestyle he had seen Roy lead, Shiv said yes in a heartbeat.

They had reached Manali early that morning and spent the day sleeping off the night of driving in a hotel they had reserved just for the day. Shiv had been curious where they would be spending the night, but Roy had assured him that they had bigger plans for the night.

Shiv sat in the driver's seat, sucking on a lemon. He was nowhere as drunk as Roy or Vikram, but it was enough to make him nervous driving at night. He could feel the buzz wearing off slowly, but he was still most definitely drunk.

Just under five minutes after he left, Vikram came to the car and crashed into the passenger side front seat. He looked excited and kept clapping Shiv on the shoulder, complimenting him on doing the job so well on his first night out. Somehow, it made Shiv more nervous than happy.

They sat in the darkness, just a few metres away from the main gate, in an alley overlooking the door so they did not block the traffic. Vikram's phone buzzed and fell silent immediately and he jumped in his seat.

'Go! They are here!'

Shiv gunned the car forward, faster than he would have liked but the alcohol made him care less. He screeched to a halt in front of the gate and right on cue, Roy came out, victorious, with a girl by his side. Shiv was confused. Wasn't the idea for all of them to get dates? Why was only Roy the one having fun? Didn't he have enough fun in Delhi on his own? He felt slightly cheated and the alcohol made his temper rise quickly.

'GO! GO! GO! Get out of here God dammit!' Vikram threw open the rear door and Roy half carried, half crashed into the back seat and laughed out.

Shiv pushed down hard on the accelerator and the car lurched forward. There was a stunned silence for a few seconds and then Roy and Vikram absolutely lost it. They started cheering and whooping like crazy and for the first time, Shiv felt truly terrified.

'What's going on here? I am confused.'

'Nothing my friend. We shall feast like kings tonight. Take it on the highway. There is a place a couple of hours from here.'

'What's wrong with the girl?' Shiv looked in the rear-view mirror. The girl was slumped over the seat, her dress in a disarray.

'Nothing. This was strong stuff dude. It hit before I even realised it,' Roy said, hi-fiving Vikram.

'Wait. You drugged her?' Shiv's eyes went wide.

'What did you think we came here to do?'

'What the fuck dude? You literally drugged her? What the fuck is wrong with you?' Shiv swerved the car to a stop on one side of the road and turned around.

'What the hell are you stopping for?' Roy yelled, looking out the window. There were still cars on the road.

'Get the fuck moving you idiot. What are you doing?' Vikram said.

'Dude! This is a crime! What the fuck man? I thought you were picking up girls here.'

'Shut the fuck up and drive. We will talk about it. Get out of here for now,' Roy snarled at Shiv.

'No. This is wrong. I won't let you do this.' Shiv replied, forcing himself to look away from the girl, whose dress had hiked up her thighs.

'Then get the fuck out,' Vikram snarled at him.

'I'm taking her with me,' Shiv said, braver than he felt.

'Yeah? I'd like to see you try,' Vikram said menacingly and before Shiv could react, he opened the dashboard and pulled a gun on Shiv.

'Done now? All your heroism and righteous anger is gone. Fucking bastard,' Vikram sneered at Shiv, whose face had gone pale in seconds.

'If you want to get out, get out here. But that is the end of the road for me. I don't want to see your face ever again. And if you mention anything that happened here tonight, I promise you I will kill you,' Roy spoke in a low growl.

'So, what is it going to be?' Vikram said.

Shiv opened his mouth and closed it again, unable to find words. He wanted to leave, but where would he go? He was in the middle of nowhere, forest on one side, steep hill face on the other and it would be midnight soon. His heart raced ahead like a race car and he felt dizzy.

'Look. It will be fine. She won't even remember anything. It is harmless fun. And it's done already. Walking away now doesn't do you any good. Just come with us and we will talk about it,' Roy offered, with a sudden calm in his voice.

Shiv hesitated. The longest second of his life. It was all what Roy needed.

'Vikram, take the wheel. Shiv, sit back. You are stressed, here, have a drink,' Roy passed him a bottle of Vodka. Shiv stared at it for a second and then took a swig.

'That's my boy. Chill out. Vikram. Drive. We are late.'

The car shot forward into the night.

Chapter 20

Shiv was woken with a start by water thrown into his face. He gasped to breathe but a stab of pain ran through his jaw like a knife. He groaned, trying to get his jaw back in place so he could close his mouth. After some grinding of bones, it clicked back into place and Shiv felt like he would faint all over again from the pain.

'Who are you?' Shiv asked with some effort. The pain in his jaw had started to go down. Maybe it was not broken, just dislocated. It was dark outside, no light in the shed. Shiv could barely make out an outline.

Shiv tried to move but couldn't. His hands were bound behind his back with a pair of pink handcuffs, clearly something the guy bought in a sex toy shop. His feet were bound with coarse rope he had seen lying around the shed earlier that night, maybe ever played with as he sat there with nothing to do.

'Sorry about the handcuffs. The last guy managed to undo the knots. Not taking a chance.'

'What do you want from me?' Shiv choked out.

'Careful now Shiv. Curiosity killed the cat, remember?' the other guy taunted.

'No! Seriously. What do you want? I can make it happen. We can talk about it.'

A slap connected with Shiv's face, making him spit blood. His jaw felt like it was on fire.

'Oh! You want to talk about it now? How nice! Yes. Let me crack open a couple of beers and we can sit, chill and bond.'

'I don't know why I am here. You just keep hitting me,' Shiv fought back tears of panic, 'How am I supposed to help you with anything if you don't tell me anything.'

'Yes. That is right I suppose. But then, you have already told me everything I needed to know. My plan is to just torture you for the night and kill you after that. Nothing you have interests me anymore,' the other guy started to walk towards the other corner where there was a heavy looking black bag.

'No! Please no! I swear I will do anything. Just let me go. I will testify against Roy and Vikram. I will even turn myself in to the police. Just let me go please. I am not a bad guy,' Shiv pleaded.

'You are not a bad guy? Let's see something,' the other guy rummaged around in his bag and pulled out Shiv's phone, 'Let's see. Aah! Here it is!'

The guy walked quickly towards Shiv, yanked his head up by his hair and shoved the screen inches from his face. Shiv's eyes squinted trying to look at it. It was him in the video, with Rashmi.

'Does this look like a nice guy to you? Someone who walks their dog? Goes out to buy milk for their old neighbour. Drugs and rapes women in his free time? Does it?'

The guy let go of his hair, and Shiv's face slumped down, tears running down his eyes now, making furrows in the dirt and blood on his face.

'You killed Roy,' Shiv spoke softly, suddenly reminded of his last phone call.

The other guy just stared at him hard, his jaw clenched. Shiv suddenly felt like he had an opening. This guy, whoever this was, was pretending to be tougher than he was. He was acting a big game in front of him, but the second Roy was mentioned, his face turned to stone, as if he was too afraid of letting emotions leak out.

'You stand here, calling me a bad guy, and yet you are a killer yourself,' Shiv said, spitting out blood and staring directly at the other guy. He thought he saw the guy squirm a little and look away.

'You stand here and pretend like you have a moral high ground, but the fact is, you don't. You and I, we are alike. There is nothing separating you from me. You are every bit of a monster I am. I at least have guilt over what I did. You, on the other hand, pretend like you are such a hero for killing someone,' Shiv pressed on, looking for a raw nerve, anything that would buy him some leverage, or at least time. Maybe, Vikram would report him missing. Maybe someone would come looking for him. He had to stall. It was his only shot.

'He deserved to die,' the other guy said, still looking away.

'Who are you to decide that? What gives you the right to sentence someone to death? Sure, he was a criminal and absolute scum of the Earth, but then what are you? Killing him does not make you a hero, it only makes you a killer. You are a murderer, and sure, you have me tied and beaten up here, but don't think you are better than any of us. You and I are the same.'

'No! We are not the same!' He roared.

Shiv forced out a laugh, even though his paining jaw made stars spin in front of his eyes. He had managed to hit a nerve. He just had to press now.

'Yes, we are! Rashmi's death was an accident. It was never meant to go that way. Things just got out of hand and before we even realised what had happened, it was all done. But you. You killed Roy. You planned the murder. You are right. We are not the same. You are worse than us.'

'What do you mean Rashmi's death was an accident?' the other guy spoke, looking at him with an expressionless face.

Shiv paused. Images from the night flooded in front of his eyes and his breathing quickened. Thinking about the night still gave him panic attacks. He took a few deep breaths to get his heartbeat under control and gestured towards the *matka* in the corner. The other guy rose and gave him some water, Shiv drank greedily, the water carving a cold route down his chest. He rinsed his mouth and spat out blood and started talking.

Chapter 21

Manali
A Year Ago

It was just about three in the night. Shiv sat there in the chair, motionless, the reality of what had happened dawning on him steadily as he sobered up. He had been an accomplice in a gangrape. They had drugged a woman and violated her. And he had done it too. He ran to the bathroom and retched, more out of panic than disgust with himself.

He turned on and stood under the shower, still naked, letting hot water scald his skin. Outside, he could faintly hear the snores of Roy, who was passed out on the couch and Vikram, who was still on the bed with the girl. He closed his eyes and tried to calm himself down. Images flashed in front of his eyes again, of the girl's limp body, her weak attempts to cover herself, trying to push him off.

It was not him. He was not the person he had been for the last two hours. He wanted to say something but got swept along. He let Roy bully him into it, coaxing him out of his clothes and onto the bed, greedily dragging him into his crimes so he could not tell anyone. And what was worse was that after a few feeble protests, he gave in. Shiv curled up into a ball and began rocking back and forth, hyperventilating, the realisation weighing on him more and more with every passing second.

He closed his eyes and turned off the shower. He could hear crickets outside, maybe a bird every now and then. Their room, in a cottage that Vikram owned on the hills, opened directly into a clearing that led to the forest downhill. There was a short bamboo fence that separated the clearing from the forest, the kind that was used to keep cattle in their enclosures on all sides. It was just the beginning of the summer and despite the late hour, the weather would have been pleasant if Shiv could notice it.

He sat there motionless for a while and then walked out, wrapping himself up in a towel. The hot shower was wearing off and the cold mountain air was making him shiver. He had decided that he would leave right away, take the girl with him. He would take Vikram's car and drop the girl somewhere safe. He did not want to speak to these guys or see their faces ever again. It did not fix what he had done, nothing ever would, but he would do the right thing now.

His eyes adjusted to the darkened room, the only light coming from the full moon outside and a digital clock on the bedside table. He stood there for a second, relearning the layout of the room. It was sparsely but tastefully furnished, with a fireplace in one corner of the room.

There was something off about the room that he could not put a finger on immediately. The room just felt vaguely bare, like there was a piece missing from the centre of the puzzle. He stood in the doorway for a while, unsure of himself, looking around trying to place what was different from when he had left. Vikram was still on the bed, snoring, his feet tangled in the sheet. Roy was sprawled on the couch, wearing nothing but his underwear. Shiv blinked, and then it hit him like a ton of bricks. The girl was not there anymore.

He panicked and ran outside to the patio. The cottage was built on the ground level and was only separated from the forest outside by a fence to keep out animals. Shiv squinted in the darkness, looking in all directions and noticed a figure in white bobbing some two hundred metres away, as if walking with great difficulty. What Shiv did next would haunt him for the rest of his life.

He raised his hand and yelled loudly, 'Hey you! Stop!'

The figure immediately picked up the pace and started walking towards the forest faster. Meanwhile, Shiv's scream roused Roy from his sleep, and he was twisting and turning on the couch, yelling curses at Shiv for being so loud. Shiv wanted to go back inside, close the door and pretend that he was driving away a fox or something like that. Let the girl go. He had been so adamant to rescue her anyway just a few minutes ago. Here she was, rescuing herself, and he hadn't had to lift a damn finger. Oh well, I was drunk too, he would tell the other two. Let them share the blame for her escape. Instead, possibilities flooded his head.

What if she remembered their names? She was supposed to be asleep till next morning, Roy had promised she would not remember anything that happened the night before. But here she was walking away, even if a bit unsteadily. What if she could identify them in a police line-up? They would all go to jail. These thoughts kept him standing there on the patio, looking at the girl running away, transfixed.

Roy, now half awake, saw Shiv standing on the patio out in the cold. He pushed himself out of the couch. It was his first time, he was a little shaken. He did not need a snitch right now at his hands. It was his idea to bring him along as the getaway, Vikram did not trust the guy to begin with. If he created any problems, Vikram would not let him hear the end of it for years.

He walked out to see Shiv staring at something out in the distance. He followed his gaze and saw a figure in white walking away. It took his alcohol-addled brain a few moments to put the pieces together but as soon as he did, he yelled out an expletive and ran inside to wake Vikram up.

Roy's loud yell broke Shiv out of his trance and he immediately started sweating through his shirt, suddenly aware of all the ways this could go wrong. He turned inside to see Roy rattling Vikram awake and pulling him by the hand to the patio. The girl was now at the edge of the forest, about to disappear into the cover of the trees.

Both Roy and Vikram got to the patio and Roy tried to jump over the railing to the ground so he could chase after Rashmi. But he landed unsteadily on his feet and immediately keeled over. He rose again and tried to run after her, but he was still far too drunk and tripped and fell over within a few feet of the house. Through this Shiv just stood there, unable to move a muscle. Everything was happening in slow motion around him.

He watched Vikram turning around as if moving through molasses, walking to the bedside drawer and pulling out a gun. Vikram stumbled back and before Shiv could realise what was happening, raised the gun in the air and fired. The shot was deafening out in the wilderness and for a second Shiv vaguely wondered if this could trigger a landslide. The figure running away in white hesitated for a second and then broke into a hobbling sprint, clearly injured in one foot.

Shiv saw Vikram shrug and bring his hand down, holding his right wrist with his left to steady his shot and close one eye. He tilted his head to the side, blinked rapidly and took aim. Shiv was horrified at the realisation of what was about to happen. He lunged at Vikram, yelling 'NO'. He tugged at his arm and made the bullet he had harmlessly go bury itself in the ground some twenty feet away from them, splattering them with dust. Vikram turned around, his face lined in fury and punched Shiv right on his left temple. Shiv reeled from the hit and fell, his eyes swimming with water.

Like staring through a dirty glass, he saw Vikram raise his shooting arm again and start to take aim. Roy was still lying sprawled on the ground, crawling more than walking. Shiv yelled in anger and lunged again, trying to catch Vikram by the arm and pull him down to the floor. Vikram saw him coming and decided he would not have enough time to aim and started to squeeze the trigger. At the last moment, just before the hammer would fall, Shiv reached Vikram and tugged at his hand, lowering it to the ground. BANG! The bullet exploded and from the corner of his eye, Shiv noticed the figure in white disappearing into the ground. Time slowed around him, as his heart jumped to his mouth.

'You Jackass! Look what you made me do. I was aiming for her legs, you moron. I don't know where she got hit now. Her death, it's on you motherfucker,' Vikram roared.

'She is dead?' Shiv asked, his voice trembling.

'I saw it. It hit her in the head. She went down in a heap,' Roy replied slowly.

'You are the one holding the gun, you fucking freak. You can't walk and you expect me to fucking think you can aim and shoot at her legs. Fuck off!' Shiv exploded back.

'Guys,' Roy intervened, 'Let's go look for her then. We can't leave behind a body. We will have to deal with it.'

'Jesus Christ! Listen to yourself, you goddamn psychopaths. You just killed someone and here you are, standing around planning to get rid of her body. You monsters, I should have never gotten into the car with you.'

'Fuck off! I didn't hear you complain when you were fucking her. Don't give me this holier than thou bullshit. You are every bit involved as we are. We are just not utterly useless in a crisis, running around like a headless chicken,' Roy shot back.

'Yeah. Fine. Fuckface, go look for the body. We will join you in a minute,' Vikram tried to get Roy to calm down a bit.

'Why am I going? You shot her!' Shiv yelled in impotent rage.

'Well, I need to suck on a lemon first you idiot. I can barely stay up. Get out there and fucking find her body or else we are all dead.'

Shiv felt the blood drain from her body in an instant. They raped and killed someone. He had raped and killed someone. He was one of the guys he would read about in the newspaper. He retched over the railing, in panic, in fear, in disgust. He could feel himself going into shock, his head reeling, a faint ringing in his ears. He just stood there, tottering on the balls of his feet until a hand connected hard with his cheek.

'Snap out of it and find her! If she tells someone, we are all dead, don't you get it. We need to find her dead body before someone else does,' Roy slapped Shiv, now back on his feet and looking more in control with the adrenaline coursing through his system.

Shiv nodded and climbed over the railing and stumbled towards the forest. Roy and Vikram came soon after and they looked till the morning, going deep into the forest. But her body wouldn't be found for another month or so. They read about it in the papers and decided never to talk about it ever again.

Chapter 22

The other guy sat in silence in front of Shiv, who had just completed his story, and waited with bated breath to see if the other guy had believed him. Every nerve in his body screamed at him to do something. Fight, resist, bargain, plead, but he fought against his impulses and sat there impassionately. Silence was key. If he broke it, he could end up paying with his life.

The other guy looked away in the distance, not meeting his gaze, leaving Shiv with no way of knowing if his gamble had paid off. He just sat there, looking away into the distance, towards the corner of the room, as if trying to sort his thoughts. Shiv waited patiently for a few minutes and then finally, unable to bear it any longer, decided to speak.

'Please let me go. I swear it was an accident. We didn't mean to do anything.'

'You didn't mean to do anything?' the other guy looked up, an eyebrow cocked.

'Yes! I swear! It was an accident. We were all drunk, unstable. None of us were thinking straight. It was never part of the plan.'

'I see. So, Rashmi drugged herself and just happened to appear in your room. You didn't do anything at all. It was all her. You are the victim here, isn't it?' The other guy sneered.

'No! I swear, I had nothing to do with it. I didn't even know what they were planning. I just thought they were there to pick up chicks.'

'Pick up chicks. So easy, so simple, isn't it? Go to a bar and pick up chicks.'

'I am sorry, I didn't mean it like that.'

A slap came hard on Shiv's face once again and it felt like his face was on fire. Before he could recover, a punch connected with his solar plexus and knocked the wind out of him. As he gasped for breath, another connected with his face and nearly dislocated his jaw all over again. He heard the other guy curse and massage the knuckles on his right hand, which were red and bruised. Shiv wanted to take the perverse satisfaction that he had managed to hurt the other guy back, but he was in too much pain to formulate a coherent thought.

'Let's get something straight,' the other guy held up Shiv's head by his hair, 'there is no song and dance that you can do for me that will convince me that you are a good guy wrapped in bad circumstances. You drugged and raped her and no matter what you do to spin it, that is the truth. I have already made the mistake of giving Roy the benefit of doubt and paid for it. I am not going to do the same with you. Get this straight. You die tonight, and that is decided. All you can do is delay the inevitable by telling me what I need to know.'

Shiv's eyes snapped wide in horror and then he slumped

over. He stayed there, heaving for a few seconds, trying to come up with a plan, with an idea, something that he could use to negotiate, but came up with nothing. It was as if his brain, fighting with every neuron so far to keep him alive, had finally accepted its fate and given up. It just left Shiv with a sad sort of clarity about his senses. He could feel the air going into his lungs for the first time in his life. His eyes stayed at every spot he looked at, taking in things he had never thought about before like shadows and textures. If this was going to be his last day, he might as well live as much as he could.

'Alright. Fine. What do you want to know?'

'Already? I was just about to bring out the bone saw. Don't tell me you are giving up without at least a little torture,' the other guy turned to Shiv.

'I am. You win. I have no cards, no tricks up my sleeve. But I will not go away as a murderer. I know this is not much, but maybe this is my penance for my sins. What do you want to know?'

'Just like that?'

'Just like that.'

'Ok. Where do I find Vikram?'

'You will find his number in my phone. He lives somewhere in Gurgaon, around Sohna Road. Roy might have had the address, I only met him that one time. I have no idea. I have never spoken to him after that day. I didn't like him when I met him, and I sure don't like him any better after what he did. I don't know if they ever even stopped after that, so go kill him. I am sure you would be doing all of us a favour.'

'Cute, you're pretending he is worse.'

'SHUT UP!'

The other guy just blinked and stared at him.

'I am done taking this shit from you. You think I don't know what I did was horrible? I couldn't sleep for months after that because of the nightmares. I started going to therapy. Even that did not help because it was so horrible I couldn't even say it out loud. It was always referred to as "The Bad thing I did". Even in therapy. I have carried all that for more than a year now and no matter how hard I have tried, I can't run from it. Every morning I wake up and see the same face in the mirror, aware of what a monster I am truly on the inside. Just knowing that I was capable of that has broken me. So, from where I am sitting, joke's on you because I want to die. Just so I know that I will never hurt anyone ever again.'

Shiv sat there breathing hard from the effort of the screaming. The other guy was just looking at him curiously. They both sat in silence for a few moments.

'Ok, I believe you.'

'What?' Shiv blinked.

'Yes. I believe that you are guilty for what you have done. I'll let you go.'

'Just like that?'

'Just like that.'

'Is it one of those bait and switch things where you let

me go and then turn around and try to kill me once I am not expecting it?'

'What the fuck do you think this is? A Tarantino movie? That's not how it works. I can't bring down Vikram alone. I need some help. You are obviously not off the hook–I have recorded your confession and you will go to jail. But I will not kill you. I will give you the chance to testify and plead for clemency.'

'Against Vikram?'

'No. He dies.'

Shiv nodded weakly, unsure if he was relieved or scared. Maybe this was all a bluff, and the other guy had no intention of letting him go anyway. He decided to test it out.

'I don't believe you.'

'What?' The other guy looked at him.

'I think you are lying. You will kill me the second I help you kill Vikram. You are just keeping me around to implicate me in the murders, or just kill me yourself. I will not help you.'

'I understand why you are sceptical and I don't blame you. I don't know what I can do to make it better but know this. I promise you that I won't kill you. I believe that you are really repenting over what you have done, and I think that it's fine. Even though I can't forgive you, I can let you make up for your crimes. You are not that lost.'

'So… .'

Their conversation was interrupted by a loud car horn outside. The other guy held a finger to his lips and Shiv fell silent. They waited for the car to pass by. It kept honking and then, through the cracks in the grass walls, they could tell the car was turning this way. Shiv opened his mouth to scream for help, but the other guy turned quickly to him and flashed his knife saying 'Don't you dare.'

Shiv sat there silently, trying to wriggle out of his handcuffs and make a run for it but he was tied up well. There was no way he could have freed himself. The other guy rose slowly, stuffed a rag in Shiv's mouth hastily and slowly cracked open the gate to see what was outside. He then slipped out noiselessly, leaving Shiv to his fate.

Chapter 23

Aryan walked out slowly and squinted at the light. It was a large car, probably an SUV, turning towards the fields from the main road, bobbing over the stony road underneath. Aryan shielded his eyes with his hand and looked at the car. It was a dark car, a four-wheel drive that people used in these parts of the countryside to traverse the stony roads. Fuck! Had someone noticed and come to check? This was bad. Aryan covered his face with a scarf and picked up a lathi from the ground and walked towards the car.

He could see the bare outline of a man standing in front of the headlights, the high beam from the car outlining his form in a dark silhouette. The man stood there, waving at Aryan, calling him over. The car was a good two hundred metres away, maybe a bit more, on the road leading to the main road bisecting the city. The car was parked lopsided, the tires on one side of the car on the road, and the other two right on the dusty path, making the car look like it could topple at any moment.

Aryan walked slowly, banging his lathi on the ground

with each step, more for his own confidence than anything else. His Haryanvi was terrible. If the conversation extended beyond a few seconds, whoever it was, would be able to tell he was not a local. He would really be in a soup then. What was a Delhi guy doing in the middle of nowhere in the dead of the night? Drugs? Was he with a prostitute? Aryan shook his head to get rid of the worst-case scenarios running through his head. Probably it was nothing.

As he got closer to the car, he could begin to see a bit more clearly. The car was empty, no one was inside. The driver's side was open, and the driver was standing in front of the headlights, waving his hands calmly over his head. Probably a flat tire, Aryan told himself. He quickened his pace, wanting to get it over with as quickly as possible.

When he was about twenty metres from the car, the driver suddenly turned and got into the car and drove off. Before Aryan could realise what was happening, he was left standing in a billowing cloud of dust. He ran after the car, and saw it swerving on the road, took a turn to disappear. The road was left bare. The only source of light now was the moon overhead. There were no streetlights, no houses nearby. The field shone in dull silver under the full moon, every blade of grass casting an ominous shadow.

Aryan stood there unmoving, trying to wrap his head around what had just happened. He peered at the road, trying to see if there was another vehicle coming, but a blank road stared back at him. He turned around, half relieved and half confused and looked back at the *khalihan*.

It was dark but he could make out something moving near one of the walls. The hair on the back of his neck stood up and he felt his skin turn cold immediately. Someone was there, peeking in. It would be just a few seconds before they saw someone tied up inside. Aryan ran back as fast as he could, whirling the lathi over his head and shouting hoping to scare away if it was just a curious onlooker.

He could see the figure a little more clearly now, as it moved back from the straw walls and into the moonlight. It was a woman, judging by the hair and was dressed in white. Aryan stuttered for a second, suddenly afraid but steeled himself and kept on running, just a bit slower now. The woman stood there, staring at Aryan's quickly approaching figure, then turned and walked towards the thicket of trees right behind the *khalihan*. Emboldened, Aryan ran harder, making louder noises, determined to chase the woman away. The woman, on the other hand, did not seem bothered in the least and walked calmly to the treeline.

Aryan reached the wall, panting and out of breath. The cigarettes had started to take their toll. He stood there, propped up against the stick he was carrying, wheezing, every fresh breath setting his lungs on fire. The woman was some twenty metres away now, walking slowly into the forest.

'Yeah! You keep walking or I'll bash your skull in,' Aryan called out, trying his best to take on a Haryanvi accent.

The woman stopped when she heard this. Aryan cursed himself for opening his mouth. She stood there for a few seconds and then turned.

It was Rashmi.

The stick slipped out of Aryan's hand and fell noiselessly on the dirt. Aryan stumbled backwards, tripping over his feet. His face broke out in sweat, and he felt his hands get cold. Rashmi just stared at him, her hair blowing even though the night was still. She looked exactly as he remembered her from their evening together. The only difference was that her face looked pale. As if it had not seen the sun in so long. Her clothes fluttered behind her, a long, mournful trail of white on the ground that she walked on. She stood there looking at him, and then slowly raised a hand, beckoning him. She then turned, calm as ever and walked on deeper into the forest.

Aryan just sat there, sprawled on the ground, unsure of everything. He felt like he was hallucinating but the sight of Rashmi walking away did not go away no matter how many times he slapped himself. His heart skipped a beat when Rashmi's ghost raised a hand and asked him to follow her. Why would he walk behind a ghost into a dark forest? He was not suicidal. He decided to run away—as far and as fast as he could.

He scrambled away, still not entirely on his feet. He turned tail and ran. Shiv could be taken care of later. Once the sun was up. Aryan did not care if Shiv told someone. What did he know anyway? Nothing could be traced back to him. He managed to get to his feet and started hobbling away. From the corner of his eye, he could see Rashmi had stopped. Out of sheer morbid curiosity, overriding every instinct in his body, Aryan turned to take a last look. And for the first time, since their evening together in Manali, his eyes met Rashmi's, and then, a single tear rolled down her left eye.

Aryan stopped dead in his tracks, like someone had held onto his legs for dear life and would not let go. He saw, as if everything was moving in slow motion, Rashmi raise a hand towards him. Not beckoning, but a plea. She stood there with her hand outstretched, a tear tracing a glistening road down her face. Aryan tried to turn around, to run away, but found himself frozen on the spot. He started towards her, in a trance, not caring about the terror he had felt just a few seconds ago. Rashmi turned and walked deeper into the forest. Aryan followed her, walking quickly to catch up to her.

Rashmi walked at an unhurried place, almost gliding along the forest floor, noiselessly. Aryan walked after her but found himself tripping over the uneven ground every few steps and walking into branches, something that Rashmi looked unperturbed by. He suddenly felt drunk, his head spinning and his eyes losing their focus. He blinked hard, rubbed his eyes and continued walking after Rashmi. They walked for a few minutes, deeper into the forest, a few hundred metres from where Shiv was until Rashmi stopped. Aryan stuttered to a stop too, waiting for something to happen. He could feel his heartbeat grow quicker. He started backing away in anticipation, suddenly scared once more.

Rashmi stood there for a few seconds and then slowly turned and looked straight at Aryan once again.'I will have my vengeance' she said in a rasp, barely audible over the noises of the forest.

Aryan suddenly felt his hands get clammy. His pulse shot up and despite that, his body felt cold. He turned around, finally back in his senses, and ran. He could not believe his eyes, or that he would follow whatever it was he saw into a forest, and not run away from it like a sane person. Rashmi's voice rang out again, repeating the same thing, over and over again, 'Avenge me'.

He ran as hard as he could, jumping over roots poking through the floor and swatting aside the branches in his face. He ran blindly, just retracing his steps, hoping he would reach the clearing. He soon saw a bright yellow light at the edge of the treeline and darted towards it. He ran out, not looking or thinking, jumping past the trees into the clearing. And that was when he finally realised why the bright yellow light was bothering him.

The barn was on fire.

Aryan stood rooted to the ground for a few seconds, unable to understand what was going on. Bright red flames leapt high into the sky, consuming the dry straw the barn was made from. The fire roared and crackled, as if it had been burning for hours. Then a high-pitched scream from inside the barn broke him out of his reverie. Shiv! He was still inside, handcuffed to the chair!

'I am coming,' Aryan called out, unsure if Shiv could hear him over the fire and the smoke and the screaming.

'Save me! You promised you'll save me!' Shiv cried back from inside. He could barely speak, the smoke quickly filling his lungs, the rag gagging him hanging limply from one side of his lips.

The walls were all engulfed in flames by then, too far gone to break his way in. With the fire already weakening it, Aryan could not risk breaking through one of the walls. What if it brought the whole thing down? Aryan tightened the scarf around his face and ran towards the front door. It was the only way he could think of. He reached the door and saw that the door had still not caught fire. But the straw around it had and it was too hot to even get to within a few feet of the door. Aryan quickly turned around to pick up his lathi and tried to bash the door in.

'You promised! You promised I would get out of here alive!' Shiv's voice got louder and more desperate as the flames climbed. Aryan only had a few seconds till Shiv would be burnt alive.

'Just wait, I am coming!' Aryan yelled back and tried bashing the door with the flat end of the lathi, hoping to break through. The door moved a little but did not open the whole way through. Aryan swung the lathi over his head and brought it crashing down on the door. The door creaked a little and opened just enough for one person to slip in. He swung again and again, the lathi making a steady metronome click against the thin, split bamboo door. Finally, there was a loud thud as the door swung clean off the hinges and for a second Aryan could see inside clearly from the light of the flames.

Shiv's trouser legs had caught fire, and he was thrashing about trying to put them out. He had fallen over, and his arm was sticking out at a weird angle, still cuffed to the metal chair, probably broken. For a brief second, Shiv's gaze met

Aryan's. Shiv screamed. Aryan stared at his pleading eyes, a cold, unmoving stare. And then, he started to walk backwards slowly, never looking away.

Shiv screamed, 'You promised! You promised you would let me go,' thrashing about with every ounce of his being.

Aryan stopped and looked hard at Shiv, hoping that he would understand what he couldn't say over the roar of the blazing fire. He wanted Shiv to suffer, just like 'his' Rashmi had. When they had violated her body, made her go through all that pain and misery. He wanted Shiv to feel even a fraction of that. Maybe being burnt alive would be close enough. Aryan hoped at the very least. He turned and walked, Shiv's screams still echoing in his ears. Aryan smiled, never even realising that he was enjoying the screaming and the heat of the fire and the pain in Shiv's voice. The screams started to grow fainter and more interrupted by coughing as he walked on, first because of the distance, second because the smoke had finally begun choking Shiv.

There would be soot in his nostrils. Any decent forensic lab would know within seconds that he was still alive when he was trapped in the fire. But there were limits to what you could find looking at a body, Aryan thought to himself as he started to walk towards his car, before the locals started to arrive. No amount of dissection of Shiv's body would ever tell anyone that Rashmi wanted her revenge and was going to have it one way or another. That was a secret that she shared only with him. Aryan smiled to himself. Everyone thought that she had died, but only Aryan knew the truth. That her body might have died, but Rashmi was far from dead. She was more alive, than being dead as compared to most people in their lifetimes, Aryan told himself.

He had not been sure when Roy had died. He had tried to pass it off as a hallucination, something he imagined in the stress of the moment. But after tonight there was no doubt in his mind that Rashmi wanted her revenge, and she had chosen him for it—a stranger she met on a hill station where they had found her body. Aryan was not going to let her down, like every other man she had known. Who rolled over and played dead, writing applications and sending letters to police that had no interest in justice. Her father, her friends, everyone had abandoned her in death, while telling stories to themselves that they cared and that they are in pain.

But Aryan was not going to do that. He was going to see this to the end. He was not going to forget, or let her down one more time, after she had pleaded to him from beyond the veil.

It was war now. He knew exactly who his Hector was going to be—Vikram Bidhuri.

Chapter 24

'What's up, hero? You don't pick up your calls? Where do you stay so busy?' Dinesh said roughly, the second Aryan stepped out of the lift—waiting on the rickety stool outside Aryan's house had left him considerably irritated.

'Sir?'

'Your phone sister fucker. I have been calling you since last night, you don't pick up only. You are too busy or what to take our calls?' Dinesh snarled. He had learnt from his years of experience on the force that these middle-class kids broke down under a stern word only. He did not enjoy hitting anyway. It hurt his hands.

'I was not here, sir,' Aryan choked out, with as much nonchalance as he could muster.

'I saw that, you asshole. Where were you?'

'I was out. At a friend's place.'

'Since when? All your food is lying here only. Why did you order food if you were out all night? You think we are all idiots?' Dinesh walked menacingly towards Aryan. To his surprise, Aryan stood his ground.

'I have the tiffin service. They deliver every night. I couldn't cancel because I did not have my phone.'

'You get your tiffin from these fancy pizza places? You are not going to admit things like this, you come with me to the station. Two lathis and you will start singing. Motherfuckers like you need that only,' Dinesh said and moved towards Aryan, swinging his baton.

'I can get you to talk to my friend's parents, where I had gone last night. Let me get my phone from inside.'

'You think I was born yesterday? I don't know what you young people do. You will just call someone and have them pretend you were there. I know you young guys very well. You were there only, right? Singh, seize his phone. And you, you come with me. We will go there directly. Even I want to see what friends these are.'

Aryan could feel his heart sinking. He was trapped. If he was caught lying even once, they would start doubting everything he had told them, and it wouldn't be long they figured out the connection between him and Roy. He quickly racked his brains and ran through every option he had available.

He couldn't go to Akshay. It was the weekend. He would probably be back at his home in Meerut. He couldn't trust anyone else from his office to lie for him either. Even if they did, it would lead to awkward questions later that he could do without. No, he needed someone else. Someone who knew what had been going on. Someone… .

'They live far away. In Noida.'

'We have a car. Come. We will go,' Dinesh said, grabbing Aryan strongly by the forearm.

'Ok. Let me just pick up my phone please,' Aryan squirmed a little. Dinesh looked at him squarely for a second.

'You think we are your servants or what? Come quietly or we will drag you there by your nails,' Dinesh pushed Aryan roughly towards the lift.

FUCK! Aryan screamed on the inside. It was all going wrong. These cops were not supposed to be here. There was nothing tying him to the scenes. He had solid alibis the entire time. He was untouchable. Yet, here they were, cops outside his house, waiting for him.

He took deep breaths, as the lift descended, trying to calm himself. All he could do was take the cop to Rashmi's parents and hope they caught on quickly enough to support his story. If they did not, he was not sure what he would do.

Straightening his clothes, he got out and walked ahead of the constable, making sure they could not see each other's faces. He debated if he should ask for a warrant but decided against it, no use making enemies until it was necessary. This guy was not Roy or Shiv. They dealt with hardened criminals daily, he did not need to pick fights where he did not already know the outcome.

He followed Dinesh, who was waiting in the front seat of the jeep. Aryan sat, facing the constable in the small bench-like seat in the back of the jeep, wondering if it was uncomfortable by design, to make the punishment start as early as the journey to the police station. He looked out, squinting into the sun, realising for the first time since last night how tired he was. The initial adrenaline had worn off and now he could feel his shoulders slump and his eyes droop. He mumbled the address to the driver and closed his eyes. Despite the lurching and the uncomfortable seats, he was asleep within seconds.

He was woken up what felt like a few minutes later by a particularly violent lurch as the jeep escaped the well paved roads of South Delhi and into the urban wilderness of Noida. Despite the tall claims of the government and the administration, there were many parts of the city where roads were still a suggestion. The further you travelled from the main roads criss-crossing through the city, the further away you felt from the capital of the country.

Surely enough, soon Aryan realised looking at the signs that they were just a few minutes away from Rashmi's house. His heartbeat quickly picked up, thinking about the gamble that he had taken. If Rashmi's parents denied that Aryan wasn't there last night, or they themselves had gone somewhere, it would all crumble down very quickly. His only hope was that Deepak would be smart enough to realise what was going on and concoct a story that did not contradict Aryan's.

The car lurched to a stop in front of their apartment's block. There was a strange power in the police jeep, Aryan realised absent mindedly. The otherwise over-enthusiastic guards, who liked to pretend they were defending the Kohinoor itself, making you jump through a million meaningless hoops before you could enter their kingdom, didn't bat an eyelid before throwing open the gates and even sent a man along, running in front of the jeep, to lead them to the correct apartment. Aryan slowly went up the stairs, his heart leaping to his mouth with every step. He stopped in front of the door and raised a hand to knock. Dinesh roughly pushed him aside and knocked on the door smartly with his baton.

The door opened. It was Rashmi's father, Deepak, who opened the door. He was utterly taken aback at the scene in front of him. Two policemen accompanying a rather dishevelled looking Aryan. Before he could say anything, Dinesh walked in, making him jump aside in surprise.

'Do you know this boy?' Dinesh asked in a rough tone.

'What?' Deepak spluttered.

'This boy. Do you know him?'

'Yes. He is Aryan. Friend of my daughter's. Why? What happened?'

'Where was he last night?'

'What?' Deepak spoke, still unsure of what was going on.

'Who is it?' Suman's voice rang out from inside.

'No…nothing. No one. You stay inside only,' Deepak called back loudly.

'What do you mean stay inside?' Deepak could hear the scraping of the chair on the floor, 'I can hear you talking to someone. Who is there?' The voice slowly got louder as Suman made her way to the main door.

She was dressed in a simple cream sari, her hair was messy and tied up in a loose bun. She had rosary beads in her hand

and was barefooted, her daily prayers clearly interrupted. She saw the scene in front of her, and quickly walked to the door.

'What is going on? Aryan? Are you ok? Were you in an accident or something? Are you hurt?'

'No, I am fine aunty. They want to know if I was here last night,' Aryan spoke as quickly as he could, nodding the entire time, hoping she would take the hint.

Dinesh muttered a curse under his breath. The guy had managed to get it out. He could not blind side the old couple with the questions anymore.

'Yes…Yes. He was here only. What happened?' Suman spoke slowly, looking very carefully at Aryan.

'What time did he come here?' Dinesh asked, realising he should have asked this without Aryan around as soon as he spoke.

'Around eight, I think? Right?' Suman looked at her husband, who nodded weakly.

Dinesh looked at Aryan, to see if he was signalling something to the couple, but he was squarely looking at his toes.

'What is going on?' Suman asked forcefully.

'He was missing the entire night. We tried getting in touch with him, but he did not pick up his phone. Then we found him at his apartment.'

'And then you came all the way here to confirm if he was here last night?'

'Yes,' Dinesh replied, puffing out his chest, proud of an investigation being conducted thoroughly.

'What was wrong with a phone call?' Suman asked, her

voice getting colder and steelier with every syllable, which was lost on Dinesh, who was oblivious to what was going to hit him in a second.

'You don't know these young people. They will call a friend and have them lie. Now that I have met you, I am convinced he was not lying.'

'Have you found my daughter's killer?' Suman said, her voice like black ice now. Deepak tried to squeeze her hand, but she shook it free.

'I am sorry, what?' Dinesh blurted out, blinking like a deer in headlights.

'Yes. You heard me. Have you caught my daughter's killers? You must have. Given you have time to travel to Noida to ask one question,' Suman turned to Deepak, 'He is the man you two met a few months ago, right? Who tried to arrest Aryan instead of listening to our complaint?'

Dinesh opened and closed his mouth, trying to find words.

'Wait a minute here,' Suman said and hobbled towards the study table tucked away in one corner of the room and fished out a folder from the lower drawer.

'Come inside. Come. Don't worry about the shoes. Please, sit down.'

Dinesh tottered on the balls of his feet, but Suman had already sat down on the couch and was waiting patiently for him to join her.

'Suman, what are you doing?' Deepak said meekly.

'You are not saying another word now,' Suman shot back at Deepak who immediately fell silent.

Dinesh slowly walked to the couch and sat beside Suman. She flung open the folder and pulled out a picture of Rashmi kept at the very top of the folder.

'This is my daughter. She went missing last year in Himachal and we found her body a month later. We have been following up with the police since then. Everywhere. Here, Himachal. We haven't heard a word from your people. Not one lead, not one clue. You closed the file the second you found the body, ruling it as a hiking accident. Who travels fifty kilometres from the city on foot to go hiking? We pointed all of this out, made appeals, begged with them to investigate further, to not close the case and dust off their hands from everything. But nothing.'

Suman paused to catch her breath. She had got louder over the course of her sentence and was now wheezing, her eyes a bright red.

'No one bothered to even return my calls for the last one year. We travel to Manali every month but still, there is no investigation. And now you show up to my door to investigate this? Do you think my daughter's death was a joke?'

Dinesh tried to interrupt but Suman waved him away.

'If you must know, yes. Aryan was here last night. You know why? Because he is helping us find out what happened to my daughter. He was up all night reading the reports and calling people who no one from your department had bothered to interview. So go ahead, arrest him for doing your job. Anyway, we know on what charges you arrest people these days. My daughter is gone anyway, take this son away from me too now. Go on. GO!'

Suman's voice broke on the last syllable, and she hid her face in her *pallu* and started sobbing. Aryan just stood there stunned. He had always thought that Suman was the one who stayed in the background and let Deepak call the shots, like most middle aged couples. But she was seething on the inside just as badly. He didn't even register that she had turned it all around and now Dinesh was the one on the stand, facing the hard questions.

Dinesh sat there silently for a few seconds, staring at his shoes. He then turned gently to Suman and said softly, 'I will talk to the SHO there. Let me find out what had happened. I promise I will do my best.'

He got up and gestured at the constables to come with him. He shook Deepak's hand, muttered an apology and walked out, never meeting Aryan's gaze.

Chapter 25

Deepak closed the door and turned slowly. Aryan was sitting on the couch and Suman was rubbing his back. He looked as if he was about to throw up, his face was pale, and he was shivering.

'Well, what was all that?' Deepak asked.

'Lay off him. Let him catch his breath at least,' Suman shot back.

'No, I won't. I need to know why there was police at my door with him in tow. What have you done?'

'Nothing!' Aryan replied, not entirely honestly.

An ugly silence lingered in the room, despite the deafening thoughts running in the heads of all of them. Deepak stared hard at Aryan, who still sat there with his head in his hands, staring at the floor, breathing hard. Suman shook her head at Deepak, still rubbing Aryan's back.

'His name is Vikram Bidhuri', Aryan said after a few minutes.

'What? Who?'

'The third guy. His name is Vikram Bidhuri. I found

him. He is a friend of Roy's. He would have his number and the address.'

Deepak stood there in stunned silence. Suman clapped a hand to her mouth, her eyes tearing up. They looked at each other, not sure of how to react.

'Are you sure?' Deepak walked quickly to the sofa and sat down beside Aryan.

'Yes. Shiv told me.'

'Shiv? You mean…?'

'Yeah. That Shiv. Shiv Tandon. He was there that night. He told me everything that happened.'

'Well, that's great then! We can take him to the police! He can tell them everything!' Deepak's face lit up. Like he could smell victory.

'What about Roy? You want to go to the police with that hanging over our heads?'

'I don't care. His death was an accident. We will tell them everything. It will be fine!'

'No! It won't be fine,' Aryan exploded, 'We still abducted him. And you may have an alibi, I do not. I was there when he died. I am not going to the police.'

'They have nothing to tie you to the scene. What are you worried about? I'll testify you were here with us, just like today,' Deepak offered helpfully. Suman nodded.

'Of course, they suspect something. Why else would they be there today at my door, out of the blue? They might have forgotten to ask me about Roy today because of their stupidity, but they will get around to it eventually. It won't take them long to figure it out if we walk in and volunteer information about two people, both connected to him. I am not doing that.'

'Let's at least talk to Shiv please. I am sure he will understand. He told you everything, didn't he?' Suman pled weakly.

'Well, we can't,' Aryan said softly.

'Why not?' Deepak shot back loudly, frustrated.

'Because he is dead!'

Suman immediately went pale. Deepak opened and closed his mouth, trying to find words. Aryan simply stared at the blank wall in front of him.

'How?'

'It doesn't matter.'

'What do you mean it doesn't matter?' Deepak spoke, getting agitated.

'Because it doesn't. He is dead. We know who the third guy is. I must finish it now. I am too deep in this. I need to.'

'What do you mean you need to finish it?'

'Nothing. I should go. I was up all night. I am tired, I need to sleep,' Aryan got up with a jerk and walked towards the door.

'Hey, I am not done talking yet. Come back here! What are you going to do?' Deepak's voice rang out behind Aryan. He kept on walking. He struggled with the latch, trying to get the door to open.

'If you don't tell me what happened, I will call the police,' Deepak threats rang hollow in Aryan's ears. It didn't matter anymore. He knew what he had to do. Rashmi had told him what she wanted him to do.

Aryan managed to unlock the door and was about to pull it open when Suman's voice rang out behind him, pleading.

'Aryan *beta,* what happened?'

Aryan hesitated. He did not care much about Deepak's anger. He had faced enough of it in his own home. He could tune out loud, middle-aged male voices with the flick of a switch in his head now. But Suman's pleas, the crying of a mother who had lost her daughter, and had taken him in as a son, that was impossible to ignore. He let go of the door handle and turned to face them.

'I know you are not going to believe me, and I don't even expect you to, but I know what I saw, and what I need to do.'

'What are you talking about?'

'I saw Rashmi again last night. When I was there with Shiv. She killed him. She set fire to the barn I was hiding him in. And she told me she wanted revenge.'

Suman's eyes immediately misted over while Deepak's face hardened, and a vein started to bulge in his forehead. Before they could respond, Aryan turned and left the house.

Chapter 26

'Very good. Now you have the one in the other hand, right? So, we put that here. What do we have now?' Kamal said patiently, staring intently at his daughter. She pursed her lips and tapped her chin with her pencil pensively, making Kamal smile.

'Twelve?'

'Very good. And how many times does twelve go by six?'

'Two times!' Ayushi chirped up, her voice bubbling with excitement at finally solving her first division problem.

'Perfect. So, write it down! So now, what is seventy-two divided by six?'

'Twelve!' Ayushi wrote it down with a smile that went from ear to ear.

'Perfect princess! See? I told you—you will get it!' Kamal pulled his daughter into a side hug. She squirmed away, looking embarrassed. Kamal sighed. How quickly these kids grew up.

'Ok. Now let's move to…' Kamal was interrupted by his phone ringing from the next room. He sighed and shook his head. Every time!

'Ok. You move to the next one. I will take the call and come back in just one minute, okay?' Kamal stood up. He smoothed his crumpled-up kurta and stretched his neck. It had been a long day and by the looks of it, it did not look like it was over yet.

'Daddy?' Ayushi said, not looking up.

'Yes?'

'Mommy is not feeling well again?' Ayushi said, not writing anymore.

'No. She is just having a headache. Don't worry about it.'

'She promised she will help me with the homework,' Ayushi said softly.

'I know sweety. She is not feeling well. Don't worry. I am here, no? We will get this done tonight.'

'I know. I just haven't seen her today.'

Kamal rocked on the balls of his feet, unsure of what to tell his daughter. He was saved by the ring, which called out to him urgently from the next room. He kissed the top of her head and walked out quickly. He wanted to take the call before it woke up his wife and lead to a whole new thing all over again.

'Yes Dinesh. Tell me.'

'I met the kid today, Sir. It's fine, his story checks out. He was at a friend's place last night.'

'So?'

'I don't understand.'

'I didn't ask you where he was last night. I asked you to bring him to the station so we could talk to him,' Kamal said, irritation rising in his voice.

'It is fine Sir. He is not connected.'

'Did I fucking ask you for your opinion? Just do what you are told, and I will decide if he is connected.'

'Sir…'

'What?' Kamal barked.

'Sir, there is another case.'

'What case?'

'There was this girl, Rashmi Agarwal, who died in Manali last year. He was at her place, helping her parents go through the reports.'

'What does this have anything to do with that?' Kamal hissed softly into his phone, afraid to wake up his wife.

'Nothing Sir. I was just wondering if we could do something about that.'

'What? It's a Himachal Police case.'

'I know. I just promised her mother… .'

'Oh my God, what the fuck is wrong with you? Are we done with crimes in this city that you want to take over cases from other states too now?'

'No, I was looking at the case, and there is something… .'

'I don't care,' Kamal cut Dinesh off, 'And neither should you. You have a case, focus on that before you start overstepping jurisdiction to take over cases from other states. Now, get to work and speak to Roy's entire contact history. I want to know exactly what he did and who he met the night before he died, and I want it done properly this time. And I want to meet this Aryan guy tomorrow, make it happen. Get me his phone records too, I want to see what he has been up to. And for God's sake, focus on solving this Roy case before you go around putting your nose in other departments' cases.'

'Yes, sir,' Dinesh replied, dejectedly.

'Good. And next time, have a better reason for calling me at home.' Kamal spoke brashly and hung up. He massaged the bridge of his nose. He could feel his migraine coming up, which did any time he went without sleep for too long. He closed his eyes and sat down on the chair, leaning back into it.

'Daddy! I am stuck. I can't solve this one,' Ayushi's voice rang out from the other room.

'Coming sweety,' Kamal called back, rising with a sigh.

Chapter 27

'Two months. If your lawyer is any good that is.' Raina replied, looking pitifully at this kid who had stumbled into his store.

'Two months? Seriously? It can't be any sooner?' Aryan asked, feigning disbelief, going through the motions. He had already done the research, he knew the procedures cold. He just needed an in.

'Minimum. That is the procedure. It never gets done in two months. You are realistically looking at six months at the very least. And even that is if you are lucky. You need some clout kid, no one just waltzes into the police station and walks out with one.'

'There is nothing you can do?'

'What do you mean?' Raina's eyes narrowed down.

'I don't know. You know.'

'This is a licensed shop kid. We don't do that shit here,' Raina growled. He knew exactly the conversation that was happening, but he also knew that both sides had to play their parts here. Thankfully enough, the kid was either smart enough to know what not to say, or so dumb he didn't know what the fuck to say.

'Ok. Ok. I am leaving,' Aryan raised his hands in surrender and walked out into the sunny lanes of Meerut.

Meerut, believed to have been a corruption of *Mayarashtra*, had always had a violent history. It was the site of the first war of Indian independence. It was the site of a British arms factory that supplied arms during the First World War as well as the Indo-China war, and home of more than thirty small scale arms factories that were set up by the government to promote industries. And then, in a moment of brilliance which can only be exhibited by the Indian bureaucracy, all these factories were shut down, leaving hundreds of highly skilled craftsmen with the know-how and without a job. Thus, began a very interesting phenomena that can only be seen in India, a cottage industry manufacturing firearms.

A few minutes on the internet had told Aryan everything he needed to know about buying a gun, other than where to find one. He knew that craftsmen from the ancient military town of Munger in Bihar were imported to Meerut to make the arms, which were sold off to small-time gangsters from Delhi, Haryana and UP to as far as Nepal. You could also buy 'second hand' World War II era guns with filed barrels making them untraceable, or he could just buy an imported gun on the grey market without necessarily needing anything resembling a license. All he had to do was hang out in the right areas of the city until someone walked up to him and spoke in hushed tones.

He had just started his day and he was here, smoking a cigarette outside the second shop he had been to. As far as plans went, his was very simple. He would go ask about buying a gun, probably get shut down, then stand outside the shop for a few minutes, and hopefully someone would come out the back of the shop. He had barely taken a couple of drags when he saw a tall, lanky guy walking towards him nonchalantly.

'*Ram Ram!*' the man raised his hands in a namaste over his head. He was dressed in brown shirt and black trousers, had a *gamcha* around his neck, and a large tika on his forehead.

'*Ram Ram*,' Aryan replied, not looking directly at him, pretending to be waiting for someone.

'I heard you are looking for something?' The tall man said in a cheerful voice.

'I might be. Depends on what you have.'

'Who sent you?'

'That is none of your business. Just know I was told to be here by someone who visits you often.'

'Who?' The tall guy narrowed his eyes. He knew everyone in the local police force. He was not one of them. Was he in trouble with the CBI? That was unlikely, the offerings had been delivered at all the appropriate places for the month. If there was going to be a raid, he would have heard a day before, so he could make arrangements. He thought hard about who he might have pissed off to warrant a visit from CBI but drew a blank.

'Tiwari Ji's son, Munna,' Aryan offered, blowing a smoke

ring. He had got the name out of the papers from yesterday. Avinash Tiwari, aka Munna, had been arrested just a couple of days ago in a hit and run case—was probably out on the streets already for all he knew.

'Oh! You are Munna Bhaiya's friend! Why didn't you say so? He should have called, I would have come to the house. Why did you go through all this trouble?'

'He has not been released yet. I don't have a lot of time. Do you have what I need?' Aryan asked, still not looking directly at the guy.

'Of course, of course. Come with me. What are you looking for today?'

'What did you say your name was?' Aryan threw down the cigarette and stubbed it under his shoe.

'I am Chhote Raina. His younger brother,' the tall guy jerked a thumb towards the shop.

'Ok. I need something small, but reliable. Don't give me shit that will take my hand out.'

'Of course. Imported?'

'Doesn't matter. I am not trying to blow someone's face off. Just need it to scare someone. But I don't want it exploding in my hand if I must put some pressure,' Aryan said a lot more confidently than he felt. The cigarette was starting to wear off.

'Of course. Of course. I have just the thing you need. Come with me,' Chhote grinned like a baboon and gestured to Aryan to follow him. He turned and started walking towards an alley a few hundred metres down. Aryan looked carefully at the billboard around him to make sure he didn't get lost. He needed to find his car and find it quickly once the deal was done. The stack of notes in his pocket felt heavier by the second.

'What did you say your name was, sir?' Chhote asked, shouting over the din of the traffic.

'I didn't,' Aryan snarled. The less conversation, the better.

'What should I tell Munna Bhaiya then if he asks?'

'He will know. Don't worry.'

Chhote fell silent and walked with his eyes straight ahead. Aryan walked behind, looking around, feigning a passing interest.

Chhote went into a small alley that Aryan would have surely missed and beckoned him. There was a row of shops, not unlike anything you would see in any other small town. Sweets, groceries, an odd motorcycle repair shop. Aryan instinctively moved towards the motorcycle shop, but Chhote stopped him.

'You also got confused, no? That is why we have set it up. Everyone will go to the metal workers for the guns, right? But it is here actually,' Chhote grinned and pointed to the sweet shop. Aryan nodded silently and followed him in.

Chhote crossed the length of the shop and went into the back room, which housed the kitchen. At the end of the kitchen there was an even smaller room that looked like a storeroom. He put the key into the padlock and twisted it open in a fluid motion, as if he did this ten times a day. Aryan suspected it was probably more that ten.

Chhote locked the door behind Aryan and started pulling up wooden boxes hidden under unfolded cardboard sweet boxes. Aryan stood around, his heart pounding, pretending to look bored. After a few minutes of shuffling around, Chhote spread out guns on an old steel table with a flourish.

It was the first time Aryan was in the presence of a gun. He tried hard not to think about what he was going to do with one. He was tempted to touch them, pick one up, try looking cool like Keanu Reeves did in his movies but he desisted.

'What are you looking at? Pistol or a Revolver?'

'Please. As if you guys can make a decent revolver,' Aryan spat out. He had no idea if they could.

'Not at all! We have the best guys in the business. You couldn't even tell the difference from the real thing once it goes off,' Chhote almost looked offended.

'Whatever. I am not taking any chances. Give me something that is cheap and will not fire in the opposite direction. Chances are I might not even have to use it.'

'Then why don't you take a dummy? It will do just as well,' Chhote offered nonchalantly.

'Yeah? And what if those guys are packing you idiot? Look if you are just going to waste my time, I can get it from somewhere else,' Aryan started to turn.

'No no. Why are you getting so impatient? Wait, I have just the thing.'

Chhote ducked under the table and pulled out a sinister looking black gun. Aryan had no idea what make or model it was but extended his hand when Chhote offered it to him.

'Got it off an army truck headed to Kashmir. IOF 9mm. 13 rounds, used by Army and Police. Number and barrel are filed so no chance of getting traced back anywhere.'

Aryan lifted the gun, trying very hard to make sure he could hold it up in one hand without showing he had no idea how heavy guns were. He inspected it, bringing it close to his eye, without any idea what he was doing.

'The safety works?' Aryan extended it back to Chhote.

'Of course. Here, look at it now.'

Aryan clicked and unclicked the safety a few times, memorising where it was. He did not want to get there and realise the damn thing won't fire.

'I want to test it.'

'Where will I get this tested in the middle of the day, sir?' Chhote grinned back ingratiatingly.

'How do I know it is not a dud?'

'You take it sir, test it. If it doesn't work, I will give you any gun you want for free. My guarantee.' Chhote said, sticking his chest out a little.

'Fine. If anything goes wrong, Munna will speak to you anyway. You know what happens after that. How much?'

'One eighty.'

'You think I am an idiot? You are not selling this to me, you are selling this to Munna Bhaiya,' Aryan snarled back. He had no idea if his gamble would work. He was simply going by his experience of Sarojini Nagar.

'Sir, you go out and find a place that will give you a better price, I will pay you back the difference.'

'I don't have anything else to do. Keep up this bullshit of one eighty and I will find another place.'

'Sir, you would get this for one thirty with a license. Leave something for us too. I have to pay to a lot of people.'

'I know everyone you pay and how much you pay. I am not paying anything over one forty-five, and I am being generous.'

'What are you saying? If big people like you haggle like this, what will we do?'

'Exactly. Give me a number and be very careful. I will either take it or walk away without a word. I don't have time all day to stand here haggling with you. So, give me one number and that's it.'

Chhote fell silent, staring at Aryan, trying to figure out if he was bluffing. Aryan stared at him stone faced, thumbing the gun.

'Fine, one sixty-five. That is the lowest I can go.'

'Ok. But throw in the bullets. I am not paying extra for that shit,' Aryan replied, confidently sticking the gun in the waistband of his jeans.

'What are you…'

'Do you want me to walk out? Don't give me the full pack. If you have something open lying around, just give me six. I don't need the whole thing.'

'Ok. You have cash?'

'No. I brought a credit card. Idiot,' Aryan shot back and reached into his pocket and began counting two-thousand-rupee notes.

Chhote turned around, looking for bullets while Aryan stood there, his heart beating frantically against his rib cage. The second he handed over the money it would become official. He would have bought a gun. Illegally. He wasn't even sure where the end of this rabbit hole was.

But then he realised he knew. It ended right where Vikram Bidhuri's corpse was.

Chapter 28

Sub Inspector Dinesh squinted at the list in front of him to decipher the next number he was supposed to dial. It was not a problem with his eyesight, that was perfect, it was the prehistoric dot matrix printer in the station which was the problem. He was sure that the thing had been bought before he had joined the force and had a suspicion it would remain long after he would retire. He had been making his way through the list of the people Roy had talked to in the week leading up to his death, but so far nothing had come up.

The friends he was with the night of his death had not seen anything different. They had gone to watch a movie and then gone to a pub and left by the time it was ten in the night because Roy said he had to go meet someone. He did not say who, so it was his job then to figure that out. All of them had watertight alibis, and Dinesh was quickly beginning to resent Kamal for having sent him on this fool's errand. He had reached a week before the incident on his list, calling people from the Friday before Roy's death.

'Hello,' a heavy, accented Haryanvi voice spoke from the other side.

'Hello. Vikram Bidhuri?'

'That depends. Who is asking?'

'This is SI Dinesh Yadav from Ramprastha Police Station in Vaishali. Did you know a man named Rohan Yadav or Roy?'

'Of course! Did you find out anything?' The voice on the other side suddenly seemed a lot more interested.

'We are investigating. I need you to come down to the police station. We have some questions for you.'

'Is there something wrong?'

'No. Just a routine investigation. We are trying to figure out what happened the night Roy died. You had spoken to him a few days ago.'

'Right.'

'So, come down to the station, we will talk.'

'That won't be possible,' Vikram replied haughtily.

'Excuse me?'

'Yes. It is election season. I am busy all day. Why don't you come to the house?'

'No. Come down to the station. We will talk here. I need to get your statement,' Dinesh's voice hardened.

'I don't think we have been introduced properly. I am Vikram Bidhuri, ex-President of DUSU.'

'So, what am I supposed to do with that information?' Dinesh replied, getting more irritated by the second.

'Do you know who my father is?'

Dinesh groaned silently. Great! Another one of these jackoffs! Just what he needed after making three hours of calls. He could remember the name vaguely. The Bidhuris were with the ruling party, held small time positions spread out over the entire family as Mukhiya or ward commissioner. Now that he thought back to it, he remembered Vikram had done the traditional student union leader stint that was a rite of passage in his family almost a decade ago and had been coasting on the fumes since. He was going to get him to the station for sure now.

'I don't give a fuck if your father is the PM. When I ask you to report to the station, you report to the station. Now are you getting your ass here or do I need to send a party to pick you up?' Dinesh said in his best policeman voice.

He had realised over the years that there were only two responses to the voice. Either the other person complied immediately or called his boss. Either way, it got the job done.

'Fine. I will be there in an hour,' Bidhuri replied after a brief pause.

Dinesh hung up the call and struck the name off his list. There was no reason why he could not have done this on the phone, but he was not a big fan of the attitude this little piece of shit was giving him. So, he was going to have him run all the way out to Vaishali, because when you mess with the bull, you get the horns.

Chapter 29

Aryan sat in a corner of the room, cradling the gun, looking unblinking at it. It felt cool to his touch, the black metal of the barrel, the texture on the grip. He cocked it back, it got easier every time, and let the barrel slide back into place. The sweet click, like that of a metronome, preparing to go off.

He raised it in front of his face, lining his eye with the sights and taking aim. He had no idea if he was doing it right, he neither had enough bullets nor space to practice taking aim. But how hard could it be? All he had to do was place the muzzle against Vikram's temple and pull the trigger.

Vikram. Vikram Bidhuri. Aryan had chanted his name in his head like a talisman a million times since Shiv had let it escape from his lips—the final piece of the puzzle. Like all things, turns out even evil came in trilogies. The Father, the Son and the Holy Spirit—Aryan drew a cross in the air with his fingers and kissed his fingertips at the end. As he waited for night to fall, he found himself wondering about what was to come, but never going beyond the night. For the first time in his life, future had an expiry date. There was no tomorrow in his plans—how he would celebrate completing Rashmi's vengeance, how he would repent for his sins.

Was he the sinner here though? Or was he doing God's work? Like avatars, who came down to the Earth when the gods could not be bothered to. Didn't *Mahabharata* promise that the saga will be repeated every time there was evil on the planet? Didn't that begin with the mistreatment of a woman as well? Arjun had killed his relatives when they erred, who were the motherfuckers to Aryan anyway? They deserved to die.

Aryan looked up at the computer, the video teaching him how to load the gun was playing on mute. He had been watching the video for hours, following along. He could load the gun with his eyes closed now. He removed the magazine and popped out the bullets one by one. He then slid the barrel back to check if there was one in the chamber already. It could not have been, but he wanted to be sure. He could not afford a mistake. A gunshot in a place like this would raise questions. The hollow tube glinted back at him. He slid the empty magazine back into the grip, cocked back the barrel and aiming at the wall, pulled the trigger. The hammer fell innocuously in place, with a click that was barely audible, so harmless, so considerate.

It wouldn't be the same once the sun was down. Aryan had played the moment in his head repeatedly, from every angle, with every possibility. Putting the gun to Vikram's temple, his chest, in his mouth. He smiled every time he pulled the trigger, his fingers curling with a mind of their own. He would enjoy the blood spurting out, maybe even splashing him in the face.

Rashmi would have wanted that. He knew it. He knew her well enough to know that she did not want to forgive her killers. She had told him herself. In his dreams, in his waking moments, he saw her face everywhere. In the mirror when he looked at his pale face, when he looked up at the ceiling as he lay awake in bed. Her voice demanding revenge would ring in his ears on a loop, until he pressed his hands to them to shut it out. Every waking moment, he would think of completing what she had started. Every time he dozed off, he would be woken up by her pale white figure haunting his dreams.

He would not back down this time. She had to get the job done herself the last two times, but this time, it would not be the same. He would prove to her that she had not made a mistake choosing him. He would pull the trigger himself. He would make sure Vikram Bidhuri was punished in this world. He would look him in the eye, tell him exactly why he was being killed, relish the fear and the panic in his eyes, and then pull the trigger. Maybe he would shoot him in the eye, or right between them, just so he could see the bullet for as long as possible. He was incapable of repentance, Aryan knew that much. But he would make sure that Bidhuri at least knew the fear that Rashmi felt in her last moments.

Cold, alone, naked, out in the wilderness, drugged out of her mind, these monsters had made her suffer. Every frame of the video had been seared into his mind. He remembered every time Rashmi raised her limp hands to defend herself, every time Roy, Shiv and Bidhuri laughed, and high fived and tagged each other in. He had not been strong enough to make Roy suffer, and brave enough to finish the job with Shiv, but this was going to be his fight. Vikram Bidhuri was going to be his prey and Aryan would enjoy the hunt.

Aryan curled into a ball on the floor, the tiles cold under his naked body. He cradled the gun and put it under his head as a pillow. He closed his eyes and imagined pulling the trigger one more time and felt the blood splatter on his face. It made him smile. He curled his finger again, and again, all six times. By the time the sounds of the last imaginary gunshot had died in his head, he was laughing louder than he had ever done in his life.

Chapter 30

Kamal looked at the list in front of him, Aryan Sinha's call records. He had gone through his file, there was nothing there. He had a driver's license application, a passport application and…that was it. He had not even had a parking ticket in all his life. He was starting to feel more and more stupid by the minute.

But there was something about the kid he could not shake. He could not articulate it properly. He had met him barely for a few minutes the first day they were investigating Roy's death and he had seemed like a normal kid. But there was just something that was off. And after all these years in the business, he had learnt to trust his instincts.

He scanned the list and there were only a few numbers that Aryan called. He picked the one that came up the most number of times and dialled it. It rang a few times, and a young sounding man picked it up.

'Yes?'

'Hello. Is it Akshay?'

'Yes. Who is this?'

'This is inspector Kamal Pandey. Do you have a minute?'

'Yes of course. Is everything ok? Was there an accident or something? Are my parents ok?' Akshay's voice betrayed panic.

'Yes. Don't worry. I just needed to ask you some questions about your friend Aryan.'

'Ok. Is he fine?'

'Yes. We are just investigating something, and his name has come up in a case. I was wondering if you could come down to the station and talk about it?'

'Do I need to bring a lawyer or something?' Akshay asked suspiciously.

'Oh no. It's nothing like that. It's more like a due diligence thing. Routine questions, nothing serious.'

'Oh. Ok. Well, I am at work right now. Can I come in the evening?'

'Of course. And I have a request for you.'

'Sure?'

'Don't try to contact Aryan please. We have him on surveillance. We will know if you did,' Kamal bluffed confidently, even though the legal procedure to get anyone under surveillance was a nightmare.

Akshay went silent for a few seconds, muttered his agreement and hung up the call. Kamal leant back in his chair and looked at the list again. Clearly these two were close. Aryan's calls to Akshay outnumbered others ten to one. But there was something strange in the list, as he looked at it more closely. The calls had reduced in frequency. Right around the time when Roy had died, he had started calling and receiving calls from one number with an alarming frequency, almost every six hours. In fact, now that he looked at the list, exactly six hours. Kamal sat up in his chair and fed the number into the system.

The small blue circle spun diligently for a few seconds and spat out a pop-up window. The number was registered to some Deepak Agarwal. Kamal pulled out his phone and dialled the number, but it was busy. He put a post-it note on his computer to call him back and started going through the list.

THE door swung open and Dinesh looked up to see a tall, fair guy with a beard and hairy hands walk in. He was wearing a white shirt and blue jeans and had sunglasses on. He was accompanied by two other men who could only be described as minions.

'Good morning, sir jee! You didn't recognise me? I am Vikram. Vikram Bidhuri. You just spoke to me,' Vikram spoke, with a smirk on his face, clearly conveying that despite the politeness in his words, he was mocking Dinesh.

'Yes. Sit down. Who are they?' Dinesh looked up at the minions, who stood there looking tough.

'Friends of mine, sir jee. They also had work here, so I thought I would bring them along.'

'Then let them go do their work. You and I need to talk.'

Vikram's face hardened for a second. The minions looked at Vikram, awaiting instructions. Vikram pressed his lips together, clenched and unclenched his fist and nodded at them. They immediately turned around and left the room. Dinesh was almost impressed by the promptness.

'Yes, sir jee. What did you need to talk about?'

'Do you know Roy?'

'Yes. I told you. Did you find out what happened?'

'Not yet. When was the last time you saw him?'

'The Saturday before he died. We had gone out.'

'Where?'

'Hauz Khas Village. He used to work in a bar there. After his shift, we generally partied there, he had access to the private area.'

'And that was the last you saw of him?'

'Yes.'

Dinesh narrowed his eyes. There was something off about the way Vikram was answering his questions. He was answering exactly what was asked. Generally, the loud boisterous kind like him could not shut up. He decided to press on.

'Did he have a quarrel with someone? Someone who had a grudge against him?'

'What do you mean? You don't think it was an accident?'

'We are looking into all possible angles. So, did he have any enemies?'

'Well, not enemies. He did run in the HKV circles so there were people he did not look eye to eye with, but that doesn't mean they would want to hurt him. It was mostly guys being guys. Fight in the night, make up over drinks the next evening. Nothing serious.'

'Think hard. Is there anyone who would want to hurt him?'

Dinesh could see Bidhuri's brow furrowed in concentration. He waited for him to speak patiently.

'No. I can't think of anyone like that,' after a couple of minutes Vikram replied in resignation.

'Well, take my number. Call me if you remember anything at all. And don't leave the town without informing me.'

'Are you serious?' Vikram replied angrily.

'I am not saying you can't leave. Just let me know so I can reach you in case something comes up.'

'Ok. Sure. Can I leave?' Vikram replied, half getting off his chair.

'Yes. Call me if you remember anything,' Dinesh replied and pulled the file in front of him.

Vikram nodded once and quickly walked out of the station, his mind racing. He found his bodyguards smoking with a couple of constables outside in front of his SUV. He gestured at them to move quickly, and they almost immediately dropped the cigarettes and opened the door for him.

Vikram sat inside and nodded once. At once, the car gunned forward, lurching over the steel grate in front of the main gate of the police station, installed to keep the animals out. Vikram pulled out his phone and began scrolling to find the messages that Roy had sent to him. How the girl's father and some guy had shown up at the bar asking questions. Roy had died shortly after. There was even a weird, incomprehensible call from Shiv in the middle of the night. Maybe there was a connection. He quickly read through them, refreshing what Roy had told him and pulled up a number on his screen.

'Hello. Guddu?'

'Vikram Bhaiya? How are you? To what do I owe this pleasure?'

'You have contacts in the Manali Police Station?'

'Not off the top of my head, but I can find someone. Why? What do you need?'

'If it was just Roy, it probably wouldn't have meant anything. But after that call from Shiv, I can't take a chance. I need you to do something for me. Pull up your contact there. I need the information of the family of an old case there.'

'Sure. I think I can do that. What do you need?'

'Find where the father lives. And get me the phone number too.'

'Ok. What is the case?'

'Rashmi Agarwal.'

Chapter 31

Akshay knocked on the door weakly, half hoping no one would reply. It was late in the day, nearly eight. If Bollywood movies were worth anything he knew that police officers weren't the hardest workers around and would not be found around at that time. The movies failed him though. A sharp "Come in" floated out from behind the closed door. He took a deep breath in and pushed the door open.

Kamal Pandey was sitting at his desk, going through his files for the day. Witness testimonies, forensic reports, copies of bills and invoices proving alibis. Unlike what most people liked to treat them as, 'files' were not a monolith, a magical artifact that bestowed wisdom on anyone who cared to look inside. They were just a chaotic collection of information, much of which had nothing to do with what was important. It needed a trained eye to identify what was in there.

Take this kid for instance, Kamal thought to himself looking up. Well dressed, expensive shoes, nervous. He would not be a challenge. He would tell Kamal exactly what he needed to know as long as he asked the questions smartly.

Let him volunteer the information, pretend to know more than he did. He was not a hardened criminal. It was an upper middle-class kid scared shitless by the mere presence of the not so pretty parts of the world he wandered through cluelessly.

'Akshay? Please sit down. Do you want something—tea or do you young people drink coffee these days?' Kamal offered with a smile. Like taking candy from a kid.

'No, I am fine, thank you. What is it about?'

'Nothing. We were investigating a case, and I was wondering if you could help me out with something.'

'Sure, of course. Whatever you need,' Akshay smiled back nervously, unsure of what to do. He had tried speaking to Aryan, but he had not picked up his cell, or opened the door when he went to his house.

'Now, do you know him?' Kamal put a picture in front of Akshay. He squinted at the picture and nodded after a second.

'Yes, that is Roy. What happened?'

'How do you know Roy?'

'I went to meet him with Aryan one time at his club. But that was about it.'

'Ok. Did Aryan say why he wanted to meet him?'

'Erm...I don't know. He did not mention it,' Akshay gulped. Kamal knew in an instant he was lying.

'Think hard. It is very important, a person's life was lost here,' Kamal pressed on.

'Life?' Akshay looked up quizzically.

'You did not know? Roy was killed a few days ago. We

found his body in an under-construction building,' Kamal said slowly, making sure Akshay understood every word.

Akshay's jaw dropped. He had no idea about this. He was not sure if Aryan did either. They had not spoken since the day he had gone to his place, and he had shut the door on his face. He had stopped coming to the office entirely. Akshay had gone to his place a couple of times after that, but Aryan was never home. He wanted to call Aryan very badly at that very moment because he had no idea what was the story he was to tell Kamal.

'Well, no. We went to his club one night, had a tiff with him and left. That was the only time I saw Roy.'

'They had a tiff. About what?' Kamal leant forward. He could smell motive.

'Aryan was trying to find someone who was friends with Roy. But Roy said he did not know her,' Akshay replied, trying hard to recall if something else of importance had happened that evening.

'So, Roy was not trying to sell some pyramid scheme to Aryan?'

'What? No. Aryan would sniff that out a mile away. I don't know if they ever met after that.'

'Do you know the name of the friend Aryan was looking for?'

'Yes. Rashmi Agarwal.'

Kamal quietly considered that. The name sounded vaguely familiar, but he could not place where he had heard it. He shook his head clear to focus on the matter at hand.

So, Aryan had lied to him after all. Which meant the night after Roy's death, he was there at his house, and not to talk business. He pulled out his phone.

'Ok, you can leave now. Thank you very much. It was extremely helpful. We will get back in touch if we need anything else.'

Akshay sat there confused for a second, until he realised that he had been dismissed and was free to go. He nodded his thanks silently and walked out of the room. He made up his mind to go meet Aryan right that minute and figure out what on Earth was going on, no matter what he had to do.

Kamal waited till Akshay was out of earshot and called up Dinesh. He wanted Aryan brought in.

'Dinesh, what did I tell you? This Aryan kid was sketchy. He lied to us that day. He wasn't there at Roy's place to talk about business. He had already had a fight with him a few days ago, looking for a friend. I knew it!'

'Oh!'

'Yes. I am going to bring him in. Send me his address and meet me there.'

'Shouldn't we wait for a warrant?'

'I am only bringing him in for questioning. It is not an arrest. Let me talk to him, see if he gives me something, and then arrest him based on that.'

'Ok. I spoke to Roy's contact list too. Nothing significant there.'

'It's ok. I am sure this kid will give us something to go by. Meet me there.'

'Ok.'

Kamal hung up the call and stared at the phone, looking at the time glinting back at him on the black screen. It was late in the night and his driver wasn't around. It was close, from what he remembered, nothing he could not manage. He hoped to wrap this all up and get home before ten that night to tuck Ayushi in for a change.

Chapter 32

'Open the damn door Aryan, I am not leaving until you do!' Akshay practically broke the door down. This whole thing had gone on for way too long. This was getting out of hand now, the secrecy, avoiding him, and now he was involved with the police!

Akshay stopped banging the door to listen closely. He could hear feet shuffling inside, even though the lights were all out. He felt blood rising to his temples.

'I can hear you inside, you asshole. Open the fuck up or I will call the inspector who was asking about you right now and have him…'

His threat wasn't even complete when Aryan jerked the door open and pulled Akshay inside by the collar. He roughly shoved Akshay inside and closed the door, staring out the eyehole, his breath stuck in his chest.

It took Akshay a minute to get used to the dark room. The only light was coming from the open fridge door in the kitchen. Akshay backed into the wall, looking for a light switch.

'Shut it off!' Aryan screamed the second Akshay switched on the light. Akshay jumped out of his skin when he saw Aryan for the moment before he turned off the lights. He was bare bodied, wearing only a pair of black trousers that Akshay was sure he had just put on. His hair was a mess, his face covered in an unkempt beard. And his body was skeletal. Akshay could see his ribs poking out from under his skin. He was shocked to see Aryan like this. Even at the end of weekend long alcohol fuelled benders, he never looked this dishevelled. This was almost like he had not had a meal in weeks.

'What inspector?' Aryan hissed at Akshay.

'Jesus Christ, Aryan. What the hell happened to you? Are you sick? I think we need to go to a doctor,' Akshay said slowly, afraid to make any sudden movements. He was quickly realising that the man in front of him was not his friend.

'What inspector?' Aryan yelled again, and then immediately dropped his voice and started looking around, as if someone was listening.

'It is about Roy. He's dead.'

'I know. What did they ask you?'

'You knew? Why didn't you tell me?' Akshay replied incredulously.

'What did they ask you? Tell me that first. I don't have a lot of time.'

'Nothing much. They just asked me how we knew Roy and what had happened.'

'And what did you tell them?' Aryan spoke slowly, in a measured voice, his eyes still darting all over the room.

'Just what happened that night at the club. When we went to see him.'

Aryan nodded once, went still for a second and set off like a rocket towards his bedroom.

'Aryan, what has happened? You need to tell me what is going on!'

'They know. They are coming. I don't have time.'

Akshay stood there transfixed, unsure of what was going on. Aryan looked unstable, unhinged. He was moving in quick little jittery movements, like he was on drugs. His face was pale and gaunt, and he had a distant, far away expression on his face.

'Aryan, you need to talk to me.'

'I don't have time! They are coming. I have to finish this off!' Aryan said, rummaging through his bag.

'Finish what off?'

'Rashmi. She is here,' Aryan's voice dropped to a low whisper.

'Rashmi? What are you talking about?' Akshay moved closer. He could see something glinting in the faint light in the room.

'Yes. I saw her. I saw her the night Roy died. When Shiv died. She was there. She wants revenge. She wants me to avenge her.'

Akshay felt his head spin. Aryan had completely gone off the rails. Probably a nervous breakdown. He needed help, and very quickly.

'Aryan. Rashmi could not have been there. She is dead.'

'You are lying! She was there,' Aryan screamed again, hissing like a man possessed, 'I saw her. She was there. She talked to me. Asked me to avenge her. She shows up in my dreams, telling me I need to finish what I started. I see her around the house all the time. One moment she is there, looking at me from the window and the next she is not.'

'Aryan. Aryan, listen to me. Look at me.'

'I have to, I have to finish this,' Aryan repeated, looking into his drawer.

'Aryan, Rashmi is not here. I am here. It's just me and you. Just like the old times.' Akshay said, slowly moving towards Aryan.

'No. You don't get it. She is here. She chose me. She chose me because we were meant to be, and she was killed before we could meet. She wants me to do this for her,' Aryan replied, finally getting his hand out of the drawer.

Aryan was shocked to see the gun in his hand. He did not flinch though. He could not. Aryan was too unstable to think straight right now. He did not want to set him off.

'I have to go. The inspector would be on his way. I have to finish this,' Aryan stood motionless, staring at the gun in his hand. Suddenly, with the weight of the gun in his palm, he felt calmer, a bit more like his older self.

'Aryan, whatever it is, I will help you. But you can't do this,' Akshay said softly, praying he would get through to Aryan.

'Yes. I can. I must. I owe her,' Aryan replied, still staring at the gun.

'What about me? What about all the things you owe me?' Akshay said.

'What?' Aryan looked up, and for the first time, looked Akshay in the eye since he had arrived. For a second, he was shocked to see the fear in Akshay's eyes, until he realised that he was standing in the middle of the room with a gun in his hand. This very room, where they had gotten drunk innumerable times and talked about their lives, their careers, their fears, everything. Now, here they were, so close but Aryan felt like the man who Akshay was friends with had vanished a long time ago.

'We had promised we wouldn't let a woman come between us. I don't care if it's Rashmi, but you can't ditch me like this.'

'You believe me?'

'I do.' Akshay said with all the sincerity he could manage, 'And I will help you in whatever it is you have to do. But it can't happen like this.'

'I don't know what to do. She wants me to…'

'I know. I know that. But you can't do it like this. You will fail. You need help. My help.'

'You wouldn't help me,' Aryan replied, 'If you knew what I was going to do, you wouldn't help me.'

'I can see the gun in your hand. I have an idea. But you must be smart about this. You don't want to disappoint Rashmi, do you?' Akshay inched closer. He could see it working, Aryan's grip on the gun was loosening. He just needed the gun to come to him, he could get Aryan the help he needed then.

They stood there in the darkness, unmoving. Akshay staring at Aryan, Aryan staring at the ground and the gun in his hand.

'Aryan, please. Let me help,' Akshay pleaded.

Aryan started raising his hand and Akshay stiffened. But that was interrupted by a knock on the door. Both of them stiffened and Akshay's breath caught in his throat. The timing could not have been worse.

They heard the door burst open and Aryan reacted in a split second, jumping behind Akshay. Akshay stood there in place, wanting to do whatever he could to keep Aryan there till he could figure something out. Inspector Kamal Pandey walked in, and Akshay could feel Aryan's hand grabbing his.

'Akshay? What are you doing here? I thought I told you not to get in touch with Aryan?' Kamal said in his strict police officer voice.

'I had to talk to him,' Akshay spoke slowly, gesturing with his eyes to Kamal that everything was not ok.

'Where is he?' Kamal caught Akshay's signal and immediately noticed his awkward posture. Aryan was behind him. He could make out a faint outline despite the dark room because of the light streaming in from the open main door. He quietly unclasped his holster, but the click reverberated loudly across the room and Aryan spun up, holding a gun to Akshay's head.

'I need to leave, and I am taking him with me and if you stop me, I will shoot him,' Aryan said softly, like it was the most natural thing in the World.

'Son, put the gun down,' Kamal quickly gathered his wits

about himself and thought back to everything he had gone through in that one hostage negotiation seminar he had been nominated to attend. He drew an absolute blank.

'Aryan, please, put the gun down,' Akshay said, truly afraid for the first time since he had entered the house.

'You don't understand. I have to go.'

'Why?'

'Rashmi. You don't understand. I must go.'

'Put the gun down Aryan. The police will help you,' Kamal spoke in a low, reassuring voice, as he slowly inched back towards the door. Kamal was out in the open right now in the doorway and if Aryan opened fire, the bullet would not have anywhere to go other than his body. He needed to get cover without alarming Aryan, who still had the gun aimed at Akshay's temple.

'Put your gun down. I don't want to hurt you,' Aryan spoke, his voice betraying the panic he felt. It did not make Kamal feel any better. The kid was scared out of his mind. It was these kinds of people who made bad decisions and ended up hurting people.

'Put the gun down or I will shoot him,' Aryan spoke again, breaking the tense silence that hung over the room.

'You won't!' Kamal said, 'That's your best friend.'

'You want to bet on that?' Aryan snarled, pointing the gun at Kamal. Kamal knew he had an opening. Aryan would have to point the gun back at Akshay. For the fraction of a second, the gun would not be pointing anywhere, that was the time he had to take his shot.

'I just need to leave, that's all. I don't want to hurt either of you. Just let me go,' Aryan spoke, tearfully now, gun pointing at Kamal.

'Son, you are not thinking straight. Let us help you,' Kamal insisted, moving further back, towards the door. He needed to get out and lock the door behind him, or at least call for backup. He looked at Akshay, who stood there, pale in the face, with his hands held against his back. It was a terrible stance. If Kamal had been in Akshay's place, he would have disarmed Aryan with the flick of a wrist. But Akshay didn't know that. Unless…

'Akshay, tell you friend to drop the weapon,' Kamal said again, looking closely at Akshay.

'I have tried! He just won't listen,' Akshay replied, still as a stone.

'I will count to three and then I will shoot. Whatever happens after that, it is your responsibility, not mine,' Aryan said and took a deep breath.

Kamal knew this was his shot. Aryan would have to move his hand. He bent on his knees, getting ready to sprint at Aryan. The next few seconds, time slowed down. Kamal could feel himself slowly cocking his gun, getting a round in the chamber. He could sense his training kicking in, as he bent his knees to spring forward in the split second where Aryan's aim was off. He sensed the twitch in Aryan's arm as he started to move the gun back to Akshay's temple and lunged forward.

BANG!

A loud shot reverberated in the room as Akshay fell to his

knees, the support of Aryan's arms suddenly disappearing. He felt face forward and waited a couple of seconds with bated breath for the pain to kick in. It did not. He turned on his back and ran his hands over his body frantically. Nothing hurt, nothing was wet. He got up into a crouch and saw Kamal's body sprawled on the ground. He raised his head towards the door, only to catch a glimpse of Aryan running out.

Akshay got up and slowly crawled towards Kamal, trying to catch his own breath. A dark red patch was desecrating his uniform, right where his medals were. This was not one of those stories where a piece of metal stopped a bullet from going through. Shaking to his bones, Akshay put his hand near Kamal's neck, trying to find an artery. He usually depended on sensing the rhythmic pulsing under the skin to find it.

It took him quite a few seconds until he realised that he was not an idiot, there just was no pulse to find.

Chapter 33

'What happened here?' Dinesh rushed into the room, shoving the crowd that had gathered on the door aside roughly, where Akshay was kneeling beside Kamal, sprawled on the floor. He had seen Kamal's jeep in the parking lot and knew he was there. But when he saw the door open and a crowd in front of Aryan's door, he immediately suspected something was wrong.

'Aryan…,' Akshay could barely speak between the sobbing, '… Aryan shot him. He has gone mad.'

Dinesh fell to his knees and put his fingers under Kamal's jaw. It was a dead silence there. The body was still warm, blood oozing out of the wound. He could not have been shot more than five or ten minutes ago. He unbuttoned Kamal's shirt and looked closely. The bullet had pierced the sternum at an angle—one in a million shot. It would have exploded into both the ventricles and made the heart useless in seconds. Kamal could not have survived more than a couple of minutes, and that was Dinesh being generous.

'Where is he?'

'I don't know. I called the ambulance, but they are not here yet,' Akshay sobbed out.

'Look at me,' Dinesh said sternly, 'Did he say anything? Where was he going? Anything at all?'

'He just said "Rashmi", something about someone named Vikram and then ran out.'

'Vikram? Vikram Bidhuri?' Dinesh's eyes widened in surprise. It was all, by some miracle he could not comprehend, imploding and coming together in a messy tapestry—Vikram, Roy, Aryan. They were all connected. Now all he needed to do was find the link.

'I don't know,' Akshay choked out.

'Dharampal, immediately call the network company and find me the last location of Aryan and Vikram Bidhuri. Call the nearest SHO and ask him to dispatch cars to the location. I want all this to be done in the next five minutes.'

Even though Dharampal, a burly man of twenty-eight, had never met Kamal before, it was personal. You could not have punks killing police officers. It was bad for the image. He clicked his heel in salute and rushed out.

ARYAN swerved the car into a dark alley behind a triangular park and held the steering wheel so tightly, his knuckles turned white. He could feel the serrated grip of the gun digging into his palm, stuck awkwardly between the steering wheel and his hand. With trembling hands, he turned the safety on and threw the gun to the passenger seat, like it was something foul smelling. The gun sank into the seat ominously with a thud.

Aryan stared at his face in the rear-view mirror, noticing that it was streaked with tears. He had shot a man. He had just killed a police officer, someone who had nothing to do with any of the mess that he was in—who was probably a good man, with a family, with kids… .

He screamed, his head resting on the steering wheel. He was not this person. He was not a killer. He did not run around town killing whoever came in his path. He had not even killed Roy and Shiv. He did not save them, for sure, but he had not killed them either. But now it was all lost, he could not claim that moral high ground that he was not a killer. He was. He had not stopped to check, but he was sure that the policeman was dead. He had practiced the shot in his head a hundred times. He knew how to hold the gun, where to look through the sights, how to account for the recoil. It was second nature to him.

He wiped his eyes on the back of his hand and suddenly realised how cold he felt. He reached to the back of his car and found a bag he had stashed away in the car just for a situation like this. He pulled out a shirt and put it on, suddenly feeling a little more clear-headed now that the cold air was not cutting through his skin.

He closed his eyes and took deep breaths to calm himself down. He tried to recall the face of the person he had just shot dead. He drew mostly a blank, but faintly remembered a moustache, a balding head, just the smallest hint of a potbelly. But he could not be sure about any of those things. He was not really seeing. Firing the gun had been an instinct, a reflex. He did not think about it. About any of it. The irreversibility of it. The severity. He had just squeezed the trigger, the way he had done so many times in the last few days. There was nothing different, nothing unfamiliar about it. Other than the bullet, of course. And all that it brought with itself.

He could feel his heart slowing down, his breathing becoming regular. He opened his eyes to the high beam of the car coming from the opposite direction. Was it all over? Was it the police coming to catch him?

He relaxed his grip on the steering wheel. Suddenly he felt tired. Utterly exhausted from everything. The planning. The constant thudding of thoughts inside his skull. Of himself. He let his hands drop to his side. He wanted to stop. He did not want to run anymore. Follow people around. Watch them die. Kill them. He felt lightheaded and just wanted to lie down and go to sleep for as long as he could. He was done. It was over. It should have been over a long, long time ago. It was all his fault, for having dragged it out for this long.

Aryan leant back in his seat and closed his eyes. He could hear the chirping of crickets outside, the occasional whine of a car passing by in another street. For the first time in months, the only voices he was hearing were coming from outside of his own head. It felt eerily quiet to him, like someone had unplugged a radio inside his brain. He felt himself slipping deeper and deeper into sleep.

He had been out maybe just a few seconds when his phone rang from his pocket. Aryan woke up with a start and pulled it out. He raised it to his face to hang up but hesitated when he saw who it was that was calling. It was Deepak, Rashmi's father. Aryan took a deep sigh and swiped his screen to pick up the call.

'Aryan! There was a man here! Vikram. Vikram Bidhuri. He has taken Deepak, I don't know what to do,' Suman's panicked voice rang out from the speaker phone.

'What? Where has he taken him?' Aryan shot back, suddenly awake.

'He gave me an address. I will tell you.'

'Ok. I am going there right now. Don't worry. I will bring him back. I am on my way but you need to tell me exactly what happened?' Aryan spoke into the phone urgently. He put the car in gear and shot forward towards the main road leading out of the crowded heart of South Delhi.

'Vikram Bidhuri showed up at the house and took Deepak with him. He gave me his number and address and asked me to call you and send you there. I don't know what to do. Should I call the police?' Suman replied, talking through her tears.

'I have a feeling they already know,' Aryan replied darkly. His head was clear now, nothing muddled or fuzzy in there anymore. It was his mess, and he was not going to let anyone else get hurt. Least of all Deepak. It was over, it all ends tonight. Whatever the cost may be.

'How many of them were there?'

'Just him. He had a gun,' Suman replied in a whisper, as if the neighbours would judge her if they heard her husband had been kidnapped at gunpoint.

'Ok. Don't worry. You stay at home and lock the doors. Don't open it for anyone but me or uncle. I will call you once I reach there and I have spoken to him. I promise you I will bring him back.'

'Ok. Just be careful.'

'I will be,' Aryan replied and hung up the call. He looked at the navigation and gunned the car forward. He should have known. It was the same place where Roy had died. Or at least very close to it. The actual building might have been sealed off. But he knew what it meant. It was a message.

Bidhuri was telling him that he knew, and it was a challenge. Well, what Bidhuri did not know was that Aryan had been preparing for this moment for months. He would not be caught off guard, even if he did not know the layout of the building anymore. It was an under-construction building, impossible to have eyes everywhere. Too many open shafts and stairwells. The element of surprise was not lost yet. He just needed to be careful, and getting the drop on Bidhuri would not be too difficult. He was alone. Over-confident idiot, Aryan thought to himself.

It might have been a good time to realise Aryan was alone too. Awfully, terribly, more alone than he had ever been in his life.

Chapter 34

Aryan got out of the car and did not bother locking the doors. He slapped a hand on his jacket's pocket to check if he could feel the cold frame of the gun. Not that he needed to, the weight of the gun pulled down his jacket. He quickly walked towards the building; it was right next to where he had brought Roy. He squinted at the lights blinking from the top of the cranes surrounding it. The compound was lit up by floodlights and he could faintly see the shapes of workers sleeping on one side of the building under a makeshift tarp tent. He quietly slipped in from a small opening he found on the opposite side of the construction site and walked towards the building, hiding in the shadows and sprinting through the patches of light.

Aryan stopped a few hundred feet from the building and crouched in the darkness, looking around for a sign of another car. He was not worried. He had a loaded gun. It would have been incredibly difficult to shoot Vikram if Aryan got ambushed and had his gun taken away from him. He checked his watch, it had taken him just under an hour to get here.

Obviously, Deepak was safe. He was nothing but bait. If he had been the target, Vikram would have shot him at the house itself. No. He knew. He knew that there was someone else behind the screen, pulling at the strings. It was time for Aryan to end it all. Look Vikram in the eye and hope to see the fear he had seen in Rashmi's eyes, even if just for a second.

He stalked towards the building and found a staircase leading up. It was dark, not lit up like the main staircase, which gave him a perfect way to sneak up unnoticed. Aryan crouched and climbed the stairs on his hands and knees, as quietly as possible, one hand firmly wrapped around the gun in his pocket. He would peer up before every landing, wait and listen for footsteps, breathing, any sound that told him how close he was. But nothing changed the first few flights of stairs. There were no sounds, no movement, and only a faint light trickling down from some unknown floor above.

As Aryan climbed up slowly, he could feel the hair on the back of his neck tingle as the light got brighter with every flight of stairs he went up. He could tell from the colour that it was coming from a halogen lamp, burning dimly on the low voltage. He crouched closer to the unfinished, coarse stairs, crawling more than climbing, bruising and scraping his palms and knees in the process. Somewhere around the tenth floor, he stopped and held his breath. He could tell that the light was coming from the floor right above him. He waited and listened, trying to figure out if Vikram was alone. But he could not hear much. Only some very faint footsteps, coming from possibly the other end of the floor.

Aryan crept up the last few stairs, sticking to the wall, trying his best to keep his body out of sight. He stopped at the top of the stairs and lifted his head slowly. His eyes got used to the light and soon he could see a figure tied to a chair in the middle of the floor. He held his breath and listened hard. He could not hear footsteps, or people talking. It looked like Bidhuri had simply tied Deepak up and left. Aryan shuddered to think if he was too late.

Aryan pulled the gun out and thumbed the safety. It was off. He held it with both hands, one on the barrel, ready to put one in the chamber in a fraction of a heartbeat if he needed to. He stalked closer, looking all around. The danger would have come from the shadows, the person in the chair did not demand his attention. His primal instincts, carved from millions of years of evolution, kicked in, making him aware of the smallest movements in his peripheral vision. It screamed at him that something was wrong, that he should get out of there, but he overrode the fear with every ounce of his will power.

He closed his eyes and immediately Rashmi's face flashed in his mind—drugged, helpless, tear streaked. Deepak's cold, lifeless body. Suman crying in a white sari as she lost her entire family. He opened his eyes and gauged the distance. It was less than 10 metres away. He took three quick breaths and ran to the chair, coming out of the shadows finally. He had the gun trained in front of him. Speed was his only advantage here. There was no one to cover him, no one to watch his six. He skidded to a halt behind the chair and started untying the ropes binding Deepak's hand. That was when it finally hit him. The figure tied in the chair was too tall to be Deepak. Aryan stopped in his tracks. He lowered the gun, turned the safety on and walked slowly towards the front of the chair.

It was Bidhuri.

Several things happened together at this point. He heard the unmistakable click of a gun being cocked behind him. Aryan spun, raising the gun with both hands but a deafening explosion knocked him back. He stumbled backwards, his mind reeling from the sound, a faint ringing in his ears. Then another. He looked down towards his chest, the front of his shirt turning sticky and a dark brown in the low light of the building. He clutched at it, feeling the blood pour out of his body in spurts, with every heartbeat. He looked up, his eyes going in and out of focus. That was when he saw it.

Rashmi stood in front of him, dressed in all black, holding a still smoking gun aimed at him.

Chapter 35

Aryan fell backwards.

Rashmi moved quickly. She took the gun from Aryan's hands and tucked it in her waistband. She pulled out a knife from a holster strapped to her thigh and got to cutting the ropes tying up Bidhuri. Bidhuri slumped forward, his hands hanging useless as his side. Out of the corner of his eye, Aryan could see a figure walking up to him. He tried to lift his head to see more clearly, but a sharp stab of pain rose in his chest. The pain vanished as quickly as it had come, as his body went into shock, as the throbbing in his head grew louder and stronger. His vision narrowed. He could only see what was directly in front of him now.

Aryan could hear the click of a gun being loaded. He managed to turn his head. He could see Rashmi aiming his gun at Bidhuri, his body slumped in the chair, his head hanging over the back of the chair. Rashmi fired three quick shots, all in quick succession. There was no hesitation, her hands did not shake, her finger squeezed the trigger with a finesse that Aryan could only have dreamt of. She waited a few seconds once she was done firing, staring intently at the now limp body of Bidhuri.

Aryan thought he was hallucinating because of the pain. He heard footsteps on the other side and turned his head. He saw Deepak, who was working with a quiet determination, turning the chair Bidhuri had been sitting in to face where Aryan lay. He then got up, stuffed the ropes tying up Bidhuri into a plastic bag and left. Aryan closed his eyes, suddenly overcome with pain. He could feel the blood trickling down the sides of his body. He could feel the light turn darker around his face, as someone stood over him. With every ounce of strength left in him, he opened his eyes to see Rashmi standing over him.

She knelt next to his head.

'Hi Aryan,' she said softly, her hand reaching towards his hand. Aryan raised his arm, thinking she wanted to hold his hand. She gripped it tightly, then softly slipped a gun into it, the one she had shot Bidhuri with. She then leant, her lips pressing against Aryan's. Aryan could feel the soft skin pressed against his face. Rashmi's hair falling like a veil around his head. He breathed in hard, sending a sharp spike of pain in his chest and was immediately taken back to the night in the hills. All these months, he had been trying to remember what Rashmi had smelt like, and here it was—like water.

Her tongue softly traced the shape of his lips, and he opened his mouth. His throat was parched, he wanted to ask for water, but that would have meant breaking away from the kiss. He kissed back, raising his head greedily, wanting to take in every smell, every sensation of her lips against his, and hold it in his heart to the very end.

'Thank you for the phone sweetheart. I could not have done without it,' Rashmi spoke softly, so that only he could hear it. She ran her palm over his face, closing his eyes. Aryan wanted to open them again, to look at her one last time. Convince himself that was not dreaming all of this, that she was real. She was alive. But he let her close his eyes, her face being the last thing he saw.

It looked exactly like how he had remembered it. Round face. Big, black eyes. Hair that curled inwards at the end. He breathed in deeply, taking in her smell, and felt his lungs giving out. The breath would catch in his throat, as he coughed. Rashmi ran a hand over his forehead, and he could sense, somewhere in his mind, her getting up and walking away slowly. He tried to lift his hand, squeeze the trigger of the gun he was holding, but it clicked harmlessly. He kept trying, his hand too tired to raise the gun off the floor, but all he got was empty clicks of the hammer falling.

As he slipped in deeper into the darkness, he could vaguely hear what sounded like a police siren.

Prologue II

I pressed the pedal so hard that the wheels spun in the dirt like they do in the cartoons. The car lurched forward and I swerved onto the road. I kid you not, I heard a scream from behind me. I glanced at the rear-view mirror and I saw the figure in white become smaller and smaller yet running after me. I gunned forward and I am serious, I drove at a speed of about hundred on those mountainous, hair-pin roads for atleast the next hour until I found a dhaba and a petrol pump.

RASHMI stumbled and fell, watching with tears in her eyes as the car swerved away. Her shoulder throbbed, where the bullet had grazed it. She had tied a piece of the bedsheet she had run with around it, but she was not sure if that had stopped the bleeding. She breathed heavily, suddenly tired now that the adrenaline had worn off.

It took her a few moments to lift herself off the ground. She looked around, the area had plunged back into darkness once again. But not entirely, she realised. There was a faint speck of light coming from the ground in the distance. She lunged towards it hungrily, unsure of what it was, but trying to hold onto whatever she could get her hands on. She crawled towards it, her legs paining like they had never done before after climbing up the steep slope leading to the road. She inched closer to the light and realised what it was.

It was a phone! The guy had dropped his phone in his panic.

She snatched at it, relief washing over her. She had a way out now. She could call for help, she could reach out to someone who could come to her. She dialled her father's number, the only number she knew by heart, before she had even realised it.

'Papa?' she managed to croak out, despite her throat feeling parched like a desert.

'Who is it? Rashmi? Whose number is this?'

Rashmi broke down in relief the second she heard her father's voice, crying bitterly. It was over. She was safe. It was all over.

'Papa, I was kidnapped. I ran away from there. Please help me, Papa. I am so scared.'

Deepak went silent for a second and Rashmi panicked, wondering if he thought she was pranking her. But just a second later his voice rang out.

'Where are you? Send me your location, I'm leaving right now.'

Rashmi looked at the home screen and turned on the navigation system. She found the closest landmark and recited the address to her father.

'Stay there. Call the police. I'm on my way. Stay on the call.'

'I can't Papa. The phone might run out of battery,' Rashmi managed to speak between sobs.

'Ok. Don't worry. Call the police. Go to the nearest station. I will come there.'

'I can't. I am scared. Please come and get me Papa.'

'Don't worry. I am on my way. I will reach there as soon as I can,' Deepak did not argue. Rashmi was not thinking straight. Her speech was slurred, she was probably in pain, or worse, drugged. It was not a time for cajoling.

Rashmi hung up the call and walked slowly back towards the forest cover. She could hide in there for the rest of the night, shivering, covered in nothing but a bedsheet. It was warm there, and no one could see her. She was not sure she had shaken off those guys. As she had crawled away under the cover of the night, she had heard them rushing over to where she had fallen.

Despite the fatigue, the brain fog, the drugs still being in her system dulling her senses and her memory, she felt her body warming up, strictly out of fury. He must have slipped something in her drink. She tried hard to recall other details from the night. Which club had she gone to, what she wore, who she had gone with, but drew a blank on most of those counts. She closed her eyes and fought against her own memories, struggling to hold on to whatever she could. A name rang out. Roy. That was the name the guy had given her who had come to sit beside her at the bar. She opened the phone and started typing everything she could remember in case the drugs wiped her memory completely once she fell asleep. Roy. There was someone named Shiv. The third was Vicky. She was not sure who had shot at her, but her throbbing shoulder would make sure she would remember that in the morning. She squeezed her eyes shut but felt everything else slipping away from her. Did he say he was from Delhi? Or was it Bengaluru? He looked muscular, was he a physical trainer? She opened the internet and started looking online for any sort of contact that she could find.

The club photographer, her eyes opened wide in realization! While they were there, the club photographer had clicked a picture of them. He would probably tag them, sooner or later, in the picture.

She suddenly felt a sharp stab of pain in her shoulder and nearly dropped the phone. She put the phone aside and leant back against the tree trunk. There would be time for this later. She supported her injured arm with the other to relieve the pressure on her shoulder. The phone's home screen turned, and she saw a handsome face smiling back at her. She picked it back up again to prevent it from getting locked.

All his apps were logged in—Aryan Sinha. She scrolled through his emails, his messages, his tweets. In the next hour, she knew everything about him. As she saw picture after picture of him with his friends, his colleagues, his family, she could feel her anger resurfacing. He had run away when he saw her. She called out to him, begging, pleading with him to help her, but instead, he got in his car and left. How was he any better than the monsters who had kidnapped her? He did not care either if she lived or died. If he had not dropped his phone, no one would have known where she went. Maybe those guys would have found her eventually and this time finished the job.

She felt her eyes droop and felt herself slipping into unconsciousness again. She texted her location to her father once again to be safe, in case the phone went dead. Her last thoughts, those visions that you get at the edge of wakefulness, were of only one thing.

She would make them pay. Each and every one of them.

Epilogue

I slipped into a shiny red dress one November evening, just as the cold Delhi winters were starting to set in. I had timed my rescue with that in mind. I did not want to be wandering around in the freezing temperatures of Manali barely dressed and malnourished. It wasn't that difficult really. I just starved myself for a week, didn't bathe for about a month and then picked up some rags that barely covered my body to wander around the streets of Manali. It was barely two days until a woman's shelter found me and took me in. Few more days of pretending to be catatonic till they nursed me back to health. I could not give them the details immediately. It would have looked suspicious.

Once I was sure they were convinced they had brought me back to full health, I let slip my father's name. They did the rest, diligently if I say so myself. My father arrived a couple of days later and brought me back home. There was a whole scene at the shelter. Someone recorded it and put it on the internet. I became somewhat viral but just like everything else, people soon moved on.

I straightened my hair. I think it was a good performance. Papa was brilliant as the father who had found his dead daughter was alive. I think he genuinely was relieved that I would not be staying hidden away in the outskirts of the town in a shanty room anymore, paid for in cash. I went back to my room, after nearly a year and half, and found it exactly as I had left it. I suppose not making changes is not that difficult when your obsessive cleaner of a mother knows you are coming back sooner or later.

I had to do my mascara again, I had smeared it a little. Sneha showed up, of course. When Ma saw that I couldn't squeeze out a single tear even after five minutes of Sneha clinging to me, bawling how sorry she was, she whisked her out, telling her that I needed to rest. She kept showing up for a few more days, with fruits, flowers, and then, eventually, like everyone else, stopped and moved on with her life. Sometimes, during my exile, I did feel bad for Sneha. I could watch her spiral from my corner of the world, but there was nothing that I could do. I did not want to blame her for what happened, but I could not forgive her either. It was a complicated emotion, and I swung between the extremes multiple times. Then I stopped in the middle and didn't do anything anymore. I found that started coming much more naturally to me at some point in this whole thing.

I squirted a few drops on perfume on my wrists and behind my ears. If you ask the world (save two people), I had been dead for a year. I suppose it is, a tree falls in the forest kind of a scenario. If the entire world believes you dead, are you alive? What even is a 'You', really? Am I the same person that went into that club a year ago? I don't think so.

I have killed four people now, not by accident, but with complete and calculated intention. The Rashmi Agarwal of a year ago would not even imagine such a thing. So even though, my body has stayed alive all this time, has Rashmi Agarwal been alive? Or did she die that day, swallowing the drink those bastards had spiked? I often found my mother looking at me with fear, as if she did not recognise me. I suppose that was true in some sense, I barely recognised my own mind.

I painted my toenails red. The most difficult part of the whole thing had been to convince my family to let me stay dead. They wanted to go to the police, the CBI, local goons, politicians, whoever would listen, to exact revenge. I spent months cajoling, pleading, begging, threatening, hurting, doing everything that was required to get them to my side. Ma, surprisingly, came around quicker than Papa. Maybe he felt obligated to avenge me or something like that. Who knows? But I was not going to let that happen.

Ma had already lost me, in more sense of the word than one. I could not let Papa do something rash and end up in the prison too. And he most definitely would have. He didn't have the connections to sweep a crime under the rug, or the wile to cover his tracks. Maybe if it went to trial, he might have gotten some sympathy, but nothing brings out sanctimoniousness faster in the courts than someone's bad luck. The courts have learnt to offer injustice wrapped inside sympathy, under the garb of upholding the law. No, I was not going to go down that route. They were mine to take.

I put on earrings, cute little studs I have had since I was sixteen. Roy. When I had healed and had woken up after a couple of days of rest, that was the only thing I could recall from the night. The name and the ugly, bearded, panting face had been seared into my brain. It would haunt my nightmares and stroll around in my daydreams. That was where I started. But there were things to be done before I moved in on him.

I slipped on a bracelet. I started with learning how to make fake IDs. Make them myself or buy them off the Internet (bless the Russians). My parents filed a missing report for me and followed up regularly with the police station in Manali to lull Roy into a complacency, thinking the bullet had found its mark. And then, we used the fake IDs (and greased some itchy palms) to claim an unclaimed body from a morgue in UP. Roughly my age, I knew what I had worn, we dumped the body in the general vicinity after dressing it up in my clothes, for someone to discover. The later the better. It took about a month for some hikers to stumble upon it. It looked nothing like me, obviously, but my mother identified it, and it was summarily cremated to conclusively close the chapter of Rashmi Agarwal.

I stared into the mirror trying to decide which purse to take. Then came the planning. I even surprised myself. I stayed in, working for thirty-six straight hours, looking up everything there was to know about Roy and the other assholes. It took me a few months and some very helpful hackers from Ukraine to dig up their entire histories, but once that was done, it was smooth sailing. Like the dumb bastard he was, Roy had kept the video of them raping me in his computer as some sick souvenir. And that was not all, there were tons of them. Difficult to tell which ones were made without drugs, but none of them looked like a healthy sexual experience. Some were shot on a hidden camera, others after drugging the poor girl, and some with what clearly looked like blackmail.

It would have been enough to drop the sucker then and there, but it wasn't good enough. Firstly, no one takes this seriously in this country. The video would have eventually found its way to the internet, and sick fucks would have happily jacked off to it. And secondly, it was not enough to convict the other two bastards. Vikram was only in a few of them, and Shiv was in none. There was one other guy who showed up in a few videos.

I put on my shoes, lacing them up to my calves. From here, it was a waiting game. I still had access to Aryan's accounts tucked away in a virtual copy of his phone I had created. That kept me updated on where he was going, what he was doing. I would have followed him anywhere to be honest, but by a stroke of luck he decided to go to Manali again, almost exactly a year after that night.

I decided on the purse that went better with the dress. It was a piece of cake. I knew everything about this guy. I knew his favourite books, favourite movies, what he did. I even knew his speech patterns to mimic. Poor guy never had a chance. My only fear was what if he stopped trying to find me after a while. To his credit he did not, for almost a month. Kept calling my old number (I could see the call logs). I was sufficiently convinced that he could be pulled in. It just had to be done in the right way. So, I arranged (from the shadows of course) that he would end up at Sneha's and get his next lead. Easier than I expected. Everyone knows someone who knows that person on the internet.

I shoved my phone into the purse. Roy was easy. Even though Aryan had managed to mess it up, I was ready. I had a gun too, just in case. But Roy, the cinematic idiot with delusion of grandeur wanted to make a moment out of it and decided to walk to the edge and smoke a cigarette. Dumbass. My only regret was that he snapped his neck and died immediately. I had another load of bricks loaded up just in case the first one didn't finish the job.

I looked into the mirror, admiring the outcome of the night of primping. Shiv was the same. I had to step in because it felt like Aryan was going soft. I felt like he needed the extra nudge. I suppose I wasn't wrong. He could have saved him, in which case I would have had to shoot him, but he didn't. He just sat there and watched Shiv scream and burn to his death. It was rather satisfying if you ask me. Almost made me not regret Roy's disposal anymore. Almost.

I opened the cupboard to look for the last piece. I didn't even need Aryan for Bidhuri. I would have shot him myself any fucking way. You know, return the favour. But Aryan was really committed to the part. Bought a gun (no one withdraws that much cash and travels to Meerut for any other reason). Stayed basically at home the entire time, planning I hoped. I found later he also killed a policeman. Avoidable, but was out of my hands anyway. No plan goes off without a hitch anyway. I had had incredible luck so far, way beyond anything I had ever imagined. I had plans B through F planned for every step but none of them were even needed. Plan A worked smoothly the entire time, until of course Aryan killed the policeman. But hey, that didn't mess with my plans, so what do I have to complain about?

I found the small vial I had ordered off the dark web. They had surprisingly good service. I could have gotten it in any medical store too, but the shops are more willing to sell this to men than women. Now, I am only making an educated guess here, but Roy used Rohypnol that night. I researched the symptoms and they felt close enough. Even if they did not, it would do.

I pulled out my phone to several impatient messages, asking where I was. Fewer things eager in the world like a dog in heat. I replied with a dainty. *Sorry, traffic is terrible. I'll be there in twenty minutes.* It would be sufficient for him. The fourth. He was not there that night, but he was there in enough videos on Roy's computer to tell me everything I needed to know. I had known about him since almost the beginning, but I had bigger plans to carry out. Him? He would be inconsequential. Barely a challenge. Show enough skin and these guys will follow you to the end of the Earth, hoping to get some. He doesn't recognise me, though I am sure he has seen the video. I was not a person in those videos, you see. He can't recognise things.

We will have a few drinks. He will start to feel woozy. I will offer to drive him back. He will resist, but soon pass out. I know a spot. We will have a nice chat. He might be upset but he will be fine. I know how to take care of myself. He will give me more names, hopefully without slurring and stumbling over his words too much. Then he will go to sleep. For good.

My parents think I am going out with Sneha. She has promised to cover for me. God bless guilt. She will do anything I ask now. I am hoping it stays that way. I open the door and step out into the night, slightly shivering from the cold. But it is nothing.

Nothing compared to the cold in the hills of Manali when you are dressed in nothing but a bedsheet in the middle of a forest.

Nothing compared to the blood in your veins when you want to scream, and kick and fight with every ounce of your being but can only manage a whimper.

Nothing compared to the cold bodies waiting patiently on a pyre, for flames to warm them up, enough to not need heat ever again.

Nothing compared to how the dish called revenge is served best.

Cold.

Acknowledgements

One of my favourite dedications when it comes to entirety of English literature is Terry Pratchett dedicating 'Guards! Guards!' to unnamed soldiers who get slaughtered by the hero three chapters into the book. I always used to think that once you have written forty books, you are bound to have run out of people to dedicate your book to. But stepping into my measly second, I was proven wrong. No matter how many times you do it, the importance of the people around you never wavers.

The first thanks go to my parents, for their constant support. They patiently listened to my wild plans, while making sure that my feet were on solid ground, even as my head roamed around in the clouds. I wish I could explain all that you have done for me, but I can't so I won't even try.

Secondly, to Dr Shubham Apurve, for being the first one who heard this story at 1 am on some night in 2021 and telling me I should go for it. You are an incredible person and I don't know what I would do without you.

Third, to all the people who read the manuscript and gave

me their feedback on how to make the story better, Abhishek Gogna, Kriti Saxena, Ashna Sehgal, Shrey Shantanu, Divya Shikha, Uditi Gupta, Poooshkar Rajiv, Shivam Verma and Paresham Prateek. I would also like to thank every one who read the early drafts on my website's mailing list and gave me their reviews. If I am missing anyone out it is only because my memory isn't what it used to be. The gratitude in my heart remains as undying and eternal as ever.

I would also like to thank my agent Suhail Mathur of The Book Bakers Literary Agency. He was a great help in shaping this book into the final form that is in your possession. I would also be remiss to not thank Ms Renu Kaul Verma and all the gentlefolk at Vitasta Publishing. The book would literally not have existed without you.

Another thanks that are in order go to Takashi Miike, director of *Audition* (1999). Just one shot from that movie was what inspired this entire book and I would be committing gross injustice if I did not give credit where it has been so painstakingly earned.

Lastly, my final thanks goes to you, my dear reader. A book does not exist till it has been read by someone and our relationship is so closely intertwined that I can't even imagine it without either of the two parties. So thank you for sticking around as I tell these tales to amuse myself, and hopefully deriving some pleasure out of these yarns I spin.

Author Bio

Siddhant Shekhar was born in Patna, India. He debuted with the Young Adult romantic comedy novel, *Web of Ties,* in 2022. His works have been published in several national and international publications. *Join Me in Death* is his second novel. A fan of science fiction, comics and Noir movies, he is an alumnus of University of Delhi and XLRI, Jamshedpur. Though still devoted to Delhi, he lives and works in Mumbai, balancing his writing career with a job in Corporate HR. You can follow his blog at www.siddshekhar.com, where he rants about his obsession of the week or follow his social media - @author.shekhar.